THE EVENT

THE EVENT

STEPHEN M. HONIG

The Event
ISBN: 979-8-218-23856-8

Design & Production by Jennie Hefren
Editorial Direction by Howard Wells

Printed in the USA

To Laura
and the People of Ukraine

Tuesday, November 16, 2027 dawned dank and dew-laden in Bethesda. Peter Carstons showered, worked on his comb-over, wrapped a robe over his dress shirt so his eggs over easy would not drip, started a full strength pot of coffee and opened his front door in search of his *Washington Post* and his *USA Today*. He found himself staring at eight MPs. They took him into the Army van still in his robe. His request to alert his still-sleeping wife was neither honored nor acknowledged.

Tuesday, November 16, dawned warm and hazy at Fort Bragg. General Carter Burbridge was up at reveille, 0530 hours, as he arose every morning with the troops in training. Discipline flowed from the top. Power flowed from the top. Burbridge looked in the mirror at his close-cropped head and saw power. He liked what he saw. His chins felt crisp and clean after his careful shave around the folds of his flabby face. And now that Plan A was rolling, he had to admit it was all pretty exciting. The Green Berets were deployed, at the very heart of operations. And he could not wait to get to his office to read the coded reports from the Crimea. Things had been going well, exceedingly well. And the pussies in Congress had managed to keep their puny little traps shut. There were no dispatches from the embedded team, but he assumed that no problem had arisen. He had just placed his left polished shoe on the top step of the second floor, his sharp crease in his khaki trousers barely touching the top of the laces, when his wife Letitia opened the front door in response to the sharp knock and was gently moved to the side by a patrol of soldiers wearing the patch of Army Intelligence.

That same day dawned foggy and uncomfortable at the Newport Naval base; you could not even see as far as the Roads, Vice Admiral John Lefrak thought as he perused the *New York Times* and sipped his cup of English Breakfast tea. A shame the Navy had done away with those Black valets who were dedicated to serving as aides, butlers really, to the senior officers. The Navy had changed and surely not for the better. There were even ships' captains who were Blacks and Hispanics! Well, I guess there were worse things, Lefrak thought. Glancing to his right over the crisp white railing of his porch, he wondered why a small squad of Navy Seals was walking in his direction.

November 16 dawned bitter cold at the fishing camp just south of Sitka. Louis, the General's long-time fishing guide, had lit the fire in the one room cabin, and the smell of chicory and coffee boiling in the saucepan had awakened General Gregory Strykopolos (USArmy–ret.) from a satisfying slumber deep in his bedroll. Man, did the General need to piss! Now that he was, what, almost seventy years old, he had noticed that need to urinate more than any other deterioration. Hell, he could still drop down and give you thirty—granted less than a hundred, but still damned good, better than almost all men half his age! As he laced up his boots to head to the outhouse, hoping the bears had not been able to get their paws on yesterday's superior catch of salmon hanging in an allegedly scent-secure pouch from a nearby pine tree, he heard a scuffling sound just outside the door. Bear? Fox? Coyote? Taking his Browning over-and-under from the shelf to the left of the door jamb, releasing the safety and throwing the door open, he found himself face-to-face with two men in snow suits and with some sort of a badge attached to their collar flaps. The cascade of bullets killed him on the spot. The marshals were cleared of wrongdoing, as the forensic report confirmed that the deceased had opened the door holding a loaded weapon which, on examination, indeed had the safety off.

Tuesday dawned as did many fall mornings in the high plains of Texas; a chill wind fenced with the already-palpable warmth of the rising sun. Senator Julio Ramirez loved these mornings, loved to go out to the corral and watch the men work the horses, loved the indecision in the weather and in his own choice of clothing: dress for the morning, or dress for the heat of afternoon. The ranch was different since Cynthia had passed; in some ways better, he certainly didn't have to hear that he was drinking too much whiskey and "why-in-tarnation don't you shower once in a while, you're a U.S. Senator aren't you? What if someone important were to show up some day for a conference?" or some-such. Buttoning up his Western shirt against the wind, pulling his Stetson down tight to his ears, he had gotten ten paces out from the house when someone called out quietly: "Now, Julio, I want you to stop walking and I want you to raise your hands slowly over your head."

"What joke is this?" the Senator asked jovially, as he turned to face half a dozen Texas Rangers standing between the house and the decorative watering trough overflowing with colorful wildflowers. Blinking, Ramirez peered at one of the backlit figures in front and asked, "Jayhawk, is that you? Dammit, man, you made me jump."

Tuesday dawned midst stress and confusion for General Roger Heathcote of the United States Army. The General was locked in a guarded command center in Denver, coordinating a series of military and civilian-force arrests of an amazing conglomeration of people, many of whom were high-ranking military officers, members of Congress, and political operatives whose names he had overheard over the years but had never met, as they were well above his pay grade. The General had been a close friend of the President's late husband in a prior life, and when he was approached by the Secretary of State, after receiving a disturbing call from Sarah—well, she did introduce herself as "the President" which was pretty unusual from the get-go—he had taken his orders, reviewed a long list of people in the military who were not to be involved, consulted or even briefed on his orders, and had spent three days organizing coordinated actions for oh-nine-hundred hours Eastern. He sat at the command desk talking on his phones, receiving coded telex messages, and getting more and more uncomfortable.

"Excuse me," wheedled his aide-de-camp, "but can you at least now tell me what this is about?"

"Don't know myself, Lieutenant," he had replied. Oh sure, thought the Lieutenant, remembering answering several phone calls from a woman who happened to be the President. Wait till I tell the guys about this snafu, he thought.

Tuesday, November 16, dawned midst sleet and a biting 40 kilometer an hour wind from the northwest as Ivan Petrovsky stepped off the Kiev train at Kazansky Station. He glanced at the ornate arches framing the train tunnels, took the long escalators to the baroque waiting room with its ceiling murals and almost church-like feeling, and stepped out into the chill of Komsmolskaya Square. His small black backpack dug into his right shoulder; the weight of his pistol and all that ammunition made it uncomfortable. He patiently waited until the contingent from the Federal Security Service picked him out and escorted him to the car, taking him to headquarters for debriefing. Chunky and dressed in dark coats and hats, they did not speak, not even his name. Ivan had a fleeting perception that things never changed; and that the last time he was home, these same types of Cheks carried ID from the KVD.

Normally his movements were wholly unheralded and indeed even unrecognized; he did not exist officially, and to the extent he had unofficial existence, it was denied categorically. But Ivan had seen and reported things that could not be misinterpreted, at least in light of the deaths. He had been led to understand that, after a brief respite to wash up and collect his thoughts, he would be meeting with President Andorpov and some people from the United States. Whatever was about to happen, Ivan knew he was about to experience the high point of his service to the Motherland.

PART ONE

2023

1

His name was Harry Simpson and he lived somewhere in Cambridge at an address which I am sure I did not hear. He was aged 41 and had had no prior heart problems. All this he told to Doc Creeley as he lay on the front steps of my house on a warm summer night, July 22, 2023, my address then being 102 Elm Terrace in the city of Newton. He had rung the bell and my wife had answered to find Mr. Simpson seated on our top step, a chocolate-colored man in a dirty white T-shirt and baggy jeans, complaining about chest pains and asking for us to take him inside so he could rest and, perhaps, have a glass of water.

Lois shouted down the basement stairs to me—our Boy Scout Troop steering committee was having a meeting at the time—to say that she was calling emergency because of the Black man with the heart attack at our front door. Joe Creeley, whose son had long ago graduated from the Scouts as an Eagle but who continued to lend his experience to our Troop, reminded us he was a physician and went straight up the stairs, down the hall, sat down next to Mr. Simpson on the steps and began to speak with him, take his pulse, identify his level of acuity. When Mr. Simpson reiterated his complaint, Doc took the phone from my wife and told the other end to hurry, although he was not sure if he was looking at a heart condition or too much whiskey.

In retrospect, I should have known that there was something unusual, although what I might have concluded from that perception is totally unclear. Two fire engines, an EMT van and two police cars came noisily down the street from two different directions, all with lights and sirens. Ours being a quiet residential neighborhood, the ballyhoo was incongruous but, then again, you give cops and firemen noisy toys with bright lights and sometimes that is what you get.

Doc told the paramedics he suspected it wasn't the heart, as the pains were not classic, no sense of heavy weight with radiation down the left arm. The older policeman turned to the senior paramedic and said, simply, "he's ours."

"So you know this man?" I asked.

"Uh, yeah we do. Picked him up before, around Newton. Not generally out here so close, but yeah. This your house?"

"Yes it is. I'm Harding, Sam Harding."

"And you don't know him, I gather."

"No, no. He's not a client or anything."

The policeman turned away from me. "Let's get him loaded up into the car."

Two other police dumped him in the back seat of the squad, half-dragging him on his knees, one person under each armpit, none too gently. No one bothered to take his vital signs.

I was a little surprised at the rough treatment. "So you're sure he's drunk," I called out.

Someone grunted an affirmative and then the whole caravan turned on their lights and sirens and left in a hurry, heading east down Elm.

"Wonder how they were so sure about that," Doc asked as we started to go back inside. "I thought it might be alcohol, but I actually did not smell it…"

We reported the event to the meeting downstairs and everyone said "good work, Doc" and that was that. We returned to discussing fundraising. It was only later, preparing for bed, that another odd thing occurred to me.

"Hey, Lois, didn't those guys with Simpson tear off in a hell of a hurry going down towards the Center?"

"Yes, I think they did. Why do you ask?"

"Funny," I said as I pulled my pajamas on, "the Newton Wellesley Emergency Room is in the other direction. How'd they know he wasn't really ill or something?"

Of course, that was before I knew about the house on Windwood Circle. And long before I knew all sorts of interesting things about the McCabes…

2

In the laconic argot of the police, a "floater" is a body found in water. In this case, Simpson ended up a floater in the small weed-infested pond near Newton City Hall, surrounded by expensive colonials built in the '30s for the wealthy burghers of Boston. A Guatemalan gardener, soon to be deported for his troubles, reported the body one morning in August, 2023, while weeding the margin of a sloping lawn which dropped gracefully from the deck of the home he was tending.

The local newspaper reported the drowning in a brief note on the third page, identifying the person as an unknown individual who had only one item on his body which might lead to proof of identity, a slip of paper in his jeans pocket which, under forensic analysis, contained an address which was not disclosed. Of course I learned more about this, unfortunately, later on. It had been called to my attention by a couple of police officers who came to inquire if we knew the people whose home address was found in the deceased's pocket. Seems there was a police blotter entry that the decedent had been picked up at my house.

I told the police what I recalled of that evening in July, which led to a mandatory invitation to visit the Middlesex County morgue, which in turn revealed the distended but clearly recognizable visage of my Mr. Simpson. I again recounted the details of July 22nd, they took notes, but returned to my house shortly to tell me there was an inconsistent record on the police blotter of those events. They asked me how that could be. I am afraid I snapped back with a "how the hell do I know," which caused them to look at each other and then tell me that "you may be hearing from us again on this." On their departure from my kitchen, I was almost certain that the female officer, a stocky blond with her hair tied in an improbable bun, turned to her partner and said sotto voce, "wonder why he's lying?"

Later, must have been autumn by then, I was called by a person named Johnston who said he wanted to talk to me about the Simpson matter. I asked him if he was with the police and he replied he was with "law enforcement." I said that sounded a bit vague. As no further detail was forthcoming, I told him that I had nothing to say except upon request of properly credentialed police officers, and he politely ended the conversation. But that next Saturday my two Newton police officers reappeared without warning at 7 a.m., with a search warrant, and accompanied by a gaunt, gray-skinned man with mild stubble and thinning sandy hair who again introduced himself as Heinrich Johnston and now tendered identification as a member of the Central Intelligence Agency. Needless to say, I was shocked and totally discombobulated by the circumstances.

We sat, me in a robe, in my kitchen. Everyone declined coffee so I made myself a cup in my one-cup Keurig and asked what this was all about. Was there to be a search of the house, I wondered, as my son was still upstairs asleep. No search, I was told. "Why is there a search warrant?" I asked. "You never know," my favorite female police officer replied. Being a lawyer, I asked on what basis or allegation had a judge issued the warrant.

"Now Mr. Harding, you know you aren't going to be told the answer to that question," allowed my new CIA buddy, Heinrich Johnston. "I think we can move this forward most effectively if I ask the questions rather than you." A wan smile flicked across his face, revealing uneven teeth yellowed from cigarettes.

"Am I under arrest?" I asked.

"I suggest again that I be the one with the questions."

"Well," I said with the confidence of an attorney and a long-standing member of the Civil Liberties Union, "you may be asking the questions, but I'm the person with the answers. If you want to hear those answers I am going to need to know what this is all about," I said as calmly as I could although even I heard the mild quiver in my voice.

Johnston and my female officer exchanged a brief glance and then she stood, turned to the hallway and said over her shoulder, "I'll start the search on the top floor. Do you want to call up to your wife or son and tell them we are coming?"

"Okay, I got it," I said. "Sit down. Please." I turned to Johnston. "What's on your mind, Mr. Johnston?"

"Just a few simple questions, sir. First off, why did you lie when you told us that baloney about the heart attack on the steps in July?"

I tried to keep my voice even this time. "Did not lie. Ask

my wife, she was there. Ask Doc Creeley, he was outside the whole time when the police and firemen were there."

"We actually did talk to the Doctor. His story was, shall we say, not fully corroborative."

"What? I don't believe that." For the first time, my anger picked up a tinge of fear.

"Do you have any friends, acquaintances, or business with the people who live anywhere on Windwood Circle?"

I looked at Johnston, who was looking into what must have been his notes on an Apple iPad. "What did you ask? Who are you talking about?"

"Eighteen Windwood Circle. Do you know the people who live there?"

I don't really carry around in my head the street addresses of my neighbors. I asked for the names of the people.

"McCabe. The McCabe family. Caleb and Susannah McCabe. You know them, don't you?"

The McCabes. Sure I knew them. Neighbors, sometimes at our house for a bottle of wine, sometimes at their house for Caleb's near-famous salmon steak with secret spiced rub, grilled to perfection over what I always thought was too high a flame. But then again you could not argue with the finished product.

"Yes, we know them. They are neighbors. We know them pretty well. Why?"

Johnston keyed something into his iPad, passed by my question, and asked if I wanted to claim that either of them was not at my house during the alleged events of the night of the 22nd of July.

"No. I told the police before who was present. Just ask

the people I mentioned already who was there, why don't you? What is this all about? I don't get it."

Johnston glanced up at me from his notes. "Listen, Mr. Harding, a Federal operative is found face down in a pond less than a mile from your house. The only thing on his body is a piece of paper from which we were lucky enough to gather one clue, which happens to be the address for these McCabes. The police pick up this guy from your house a week before, we ask you about it and you give a cock-and-bull story about this guy maybe having a heart attack and how the police and the fire department and this doctor have him taken away in a big hurry, except there is an inconsistent police record, no fire department record, no hospital record of this happening. And your doctor says that he was called upstairs with this same pretext and by the time he gets there the only person outside is your wife and there is no one else in sight."

"Then McCabe calls the police, tells them he was just back from vacation, and asks if he can see the body that the town paper said was fished out of the drink, maybe it's one of the people finishing his basement, or maybe some guy he's seen around his house some nights, but comes down to the morgue, says it isn't one of the workers, but then asks if any papers were found on the body which the assistant coroner overhears and figures that's a hell of an odd question in the circumstances, and makes a note of it."

"Meanwhile, the computer at Langley spits out an alert that some John Doe's fingerprints from Newton, Massachusetts matches one of our people. So, Mr. Harding, we have lots of questions about you, and about McCabe, and about why someone decided to take out one of our people. And, I might say, you have not been exactly forthcoming here."

He paused while I tried to understand all the things he had just said, and then he continued: "Mr. Harding, you (emphasis on the word you) have the right to remain silent. Anything you say can be used against you in a court of law. You have a right to be represented by an attorney. If you cannot afford an attorney, one will be appointed to represent you. After hearing this recitation of your rights, would you like to try again to answer a few questions we have for you?"

I was getting the Miranda warnings which is, my lightning quick legal mind told me, never a good development.

"Sam, what's going on down there? Can I come down?" Lois was calling me from the second-floor landing.

I didn't need to be a lawyer to know that I needed a lawyer, and my cousin was with the DA's office. I called back loudly: "No, don't come down. Just call my cousin Bob and tell him I need his help. Professionally."

There was a pause. Then, "call Bobby Sherman?"

"Yes, yes. Call him now. He may be down on the Cape but do it now."

I turned to Johnston. "Am I under arrest?"

He smiled, this time more broadly. "No, Mr. Harding. Not yet."

"I have nothing to say without counsel. I have asked my wife to call a lawyer for me. If you want to search the house, go ahead. Otherwise, please leave."

Search they did. We spent the rest of the day putting drawers back into dressers, books back on shelves, covers back on storage boxes in the attic over the garage. Hot as hell in the afternoon in that attic. Turns out that the mothers of CIA and police operatives all failed to teach their children how to clean up after their own mess.

And, they took my computer. Did not know they could do that. They looked miffed when I refused them the password to my office account. After they left, I thought about telling my law firm but, for some reason, I decided not to.

At least I did not make the mistake of telling them about Caleb McCabe's conversation with me a couple of weeks before Simpson showed up dead with McCabe's address in his pocket. It wasn't until much later that it occurred to me that, seemingly, McCabe hadn't told the police about that either. Did he not know of my possible involvement in the matter? Or did he think the conversation we had in my office irrelevant or, more likely, only something that would open a whole can of worms he did not need to deal with? Guess I'll never know, I thought at the time. But now, I'm pretty sure he just decided to not mention anything to the police that would attract any more attention to his laboratory and the work going on there.

3

Ivan Illyanovitch Petrovsky pulled into the McDonalds on Route 9 in Framingham, Massachusetts, on an annoyingly chilly June morning. He went straight to the drive-through for his breakfast Egg McMuffin and a large coffee with cream and four sugars, and then pulled to the far end of the parking area and sipped deeply, letting the sweetness tingle his teeth and awaken his reflexes. The egg sandwich was still hot and an edge of white snaked out between his lips and landed gently on the lapel of his blazer. Carefully he lifted it up with the corner of his napkin and inspected the result in the mirror. No damage, his blue jacket was pristine against his Brooks Brothers shirt and solid burgundy tie. Ivan was two miles from his office at General Defense, but he had an hour or so to get there. Enough time to absorb this new envelope.

Ivan was to be Allen Parsons no longer. He would no longer live at The Inns at the Lakes, 6000 Worcester Road in Framingham. The envelope contained his new address and requisite keys, a new social security card, a new driver's license, a Newton Public Library card, an assortment of credit cards, a health insurance card and a slightly worn

United States passport with a summer visit to Paris stamped onto one of the visa pages. He fingered its stiff pages from the edges, with mild curiosity, absorbing the faintly photographic smell. His new employment would be an electronics salesman for a company based in New York City, assigned to the New England District. His phone number on the business cards was tied to the new cell phone already at his apartment. A bio of his new next door neighbor had a couple of photographs stapled in the back.

Ivan had done this before. Several times. Just disappear. No notice, no completion of his assignments at his cover work places, no last paycheck or severance. At the Inns at the Lakes one would find an empty apartment, not a single piece of furniture, no forwarding address. Just vanished. If someone had dusted for fingerprints, they would have found none. Nor any in his old office, erased the next night by the new member of the janitorial staff.

Lyle James Vincent. He was now a Lyle. And with no annoying office routine to occupy his days. Just go today to General Defense, pick up his three carefully curated items of assigned personal possessions, tuck his putative wife's picture into his briefcase along with the turquoise letter opener, slip the Ohio State diploma out of the frame and into his bag with one neat fold down the middle, and Allen Parsons would cease to exist. His car would be "stolen" that night from outside his new house, but he would not report that to the police. Why would he? A new one would be left out front, keys in the usual place.

Sixteen Windwood Circle, Newton, Massachusetts. Likely a house that blended into the neighborhood. Not too large, not too ostentatious, suitable for a businessman assigned to a sales territory for six months or so. It's a trial basis he would explain in case he had to move on quickly thereafter. Let's say the wife and kid would join from—oh, say Milwaukee, he knew Milwaukee if asked—in the Fall, in time for the next school year. Rented furniture. Gardener arranged by his company. All utilities in the name of the company. Boston Globe daily on the front walk, a couple of trade magazines arriving by subscription, matching his new employment. Very complete, very professional.

Not much other background inside the envelope with no postmark; time for details later, best to just meld into the new situation for a few days, learn the rhythm of things, the neighbors, the comings and goings. Drive around Newton, find a Whole Foods, locate the bank where his direct deposits would end up. Get a haircut; shorter this time, salesmen usually kept themselves pretty trimmed.

Ivan looked at himself in the car mirror, straightened his tie, collected the detritus from his breakfast and stuffed it into the paper bag, to drop in the hopper as he exited the lot. Don't look much like a Lyle, he thought, although he didn't think he had looked much like an Allen Parsons either. He wondered if he still looked like an Ivan and suspected he did not. He had been away so long, dormant and mobile so long without function, a remnant of a different time and reality. Only the new reality was beginning to look and feel like the old one once again. Perhaps this time? They said you would never know until you knew. Whatever that meant.

Newton was one of those bedroom communities. Families and old empty nesters. Why put a single guy, aged 36, gym buff with his hard body and six-foot-two-inch frame into that kind of setting? In the large Framingham apartment complex there were all sorts of people, and people were invisible to each other, often coming and going, in transit from one state of being and enslavement to the next. Residential upscale towns like Newton were different. There were real neighbors, real inquiries. Not that he feared he could not handle it all with practiced ease, but why be put to the bother, why waste the effort? This was the first time he was moved to such a location, so perhaps this was in fact a real situation that called for his involvement. Strange that it had ended him in some leafy bedroom suburb. No sense trying too hard to figure it out. You would never know until you knew.

Ivan was now about to run late. He turned his Honda Accord onto Route 9 and joined the flow westward towards his office. No car seemed to be lurking in his wake, but just to be sure he went into the Macy's parking lot and mixed with the other cars before resuming his trip. An old habit.

4

Susannah McCabe had been surprised when the Loftons had moved out of Sixteen. Sarah Lofton had never mentioned that they were looking, but someone had told them about a great house about to come on the market in Andover, the owner was being transferred, it was ridiculously underpriced and absolutely perfect for them. The Lofton boys were enrolled in Andover Academy and Larry's business was up in Lowell, so it just seemed too good to pass up. Sarah had grown up in Newton and really had no real interest in leaving, but the new place was just so perfect…

A week after the move, a service company specializing in relocating businesspeople had shown up, painted the north and west sides of Sixteen, put in some tulip bulbs. Then, one Thursday, Mayfair Furniture trucks had shown up, two of them in fact, and seemed to be moving in furniture for half a day. Must have filled up that old colonial pretty completely; it was small as houses went on Windwood. Might have been slated for a tear-down and construction of a much larger "McMansion" on the site, a trend all too common in Newton where open building lots were nonexistent.

Susannah and Caleb McCabe had discussed the newly expected neighbor at length. Would there be children? A couple they could relate to, share some wine, maybe grill some fish and veggies with them at the end of a long day? Surely whoever was moving in had some dollars to spare, or at least their company did. The lawn had been cut and the bushes trimmed. The leaves and waste had been expertly cleaned out by Santori Brothers, known as the best (and most expensive) gardening company in Newton.

Caleb hoped for a couple who could play bridge, had some social awareness, and also with one member possessing some scientific curiosity. His work at the Harvard Biological Research Annex was his consuming passion, and even though it had become mostly classified, it would be nice to have a technical conversation once in a while, away from the lab, with a neighbor who knew the difference between large and small molecules. Susannah had majored in French literature and had no card sense, but then again that was not much of an indictment given the vagaries of human nature. He felt himself, on balance, a lucky guy. The boys were cool, and there were good science laboratories at Newton Prep. He had made it a point to check before swallowing hard and agreeing to enroll each of them at 50K a year.

Then, one morning, there was this tall guy in jeans picking up a paper from the walkway, glancing around and walking into Sixteen. A Lexus sat in the driveway. The new neighbors seemingly had arrived. Caleb had an urge to call out, or walk over, but thought better of it. Best not to rush people, particularly before they had their morning coffee. He went upstairs, kissed Susannah as she stirred in bed, mentioned that there were people in Sixteen and he was off to work. Susannah made to pucker, rolled over and fell back asleep.

Lyle, ensconced in Sixteen Windwood, propped his paper up next to his coffee mug and waited for it to cool. Italian blend, strong enough to taste tolerable coming out of a coffee machine that was not an espresso steam engine. He was sitting in the front den, angled toward the street with a pretty clear view of the McCabe house at Eighteen. He thought he saw a middle-aged guy with a balding head and an incongruous soul patch looking out when Lyle had picked up his paper. Then a light had gone on upstairs for a moment in a corner room, likely the master bedroom, then out again. Baldy, must be this Caleb, looked like the photograph although the guy was a hundred feet away and moving briskly. He got into an old Chevy and drove off. No doubt to the Harvard Bio Research Annex. It was a work day and Lyle had checked out the parking stickers on the car the prior evening when out for a walk.

The McCabe boys had left for summer day camp in a small van much earlier. With the light on and off upstairs, Lyle guessed Susannah was still in bed and had gotten a quick good-bye. Why Caleb had turned on the light he could not say. Habit perhaps, or perhaps Susannah was worth a careful look.

Lyle skimmed the *Boston Globe*. Red Sox were winning, Congress was deadlocked on Iran, ISIS was losing and winning cities with Arabic names. Lyle kept up with sports to fit in, he kept up with world events because that once was, and in a way still was, his true business. On page 5, Putin was belittling U.S. sanctions on Russian businesses, his grim unlined face looking particularly flat and menacing in the small black and white photograph, with some men in military uniforms standing behind him. Lyle wasn't sure how Putin ended up in charge, but he was trained to follow the office, not the man, and to keep focus on the Motherland, not on the temporary holder of power. Lyle thought for an instant about St. Petersburg, the pastel houses diffusing into the early morning air, the city relaxed and confident that it was more permanent than any government which temporarily, however completely, ruled over it.

He flipped to the television listings and spent a few minutes. Lyle never watched very much television even though each residence always was equipped with a large high definition screen. Just like knowing the Red Sox players in Boston, you had to know about the programming if you wanted to be accepted as American. And Lyle always needed to blend, right down to his Chuck Taylors and his flat Midwestern accent. Actually, if you thought about it, not really an accent at all, just plain-spoken English as if you were born and raised—well, somewhere you couldn't quite put your finger on.

Maybe this relocation was just the same old thing: be available. Surely nothing was more boring than being available. But the hardest part was the women. Lyle liked women and women liked Lyle, but you had to avoid involvements, questions, answers, anything permanent. That led to a smorgasbord of experiences, not all that bad, but sometimes he thought that at some point he would like something more. The thought that "more" might end up being located in the United States always brought him up short, however. It was not really what his soul had in mind, even if other bodily elements were willing to consider it. Never signed up for this, he thought, but then resisted a mental definition of "this."

A trim middle-aged woman, blonde going to white overtones interspersed with the drying grayness of approaching 50, came out of Eighteen. Lyle got up quickly, hurried to the front door, then ambled out slowly, stopping at the end of his front walk and looking around. The woman put down her gardening gloves, self-consciously pushed downward on the outside seams of her tan shorts with her bare palms, looked over and smiled tentatively. He smiled back with a half-nod, then slowly turned and headed down the street, away from Eighteen. Slow, slow, slow. Slow was always faster in the end. When you pushed something, you made little rips in the fabric of your persona, and in the long run they sometimes opened into long gashes you needed to cauterize. Real people often went slow because they weren't going anywhere in particular. That is what Lyle was practiced in doing. He walked down Windwood towards Main Street, swinging his arms, not a care or an agenda in the world.

5

Brianna squinted tightly. The disinfectant was almost but not quite completely eyes-friendly. The fluids gently ran over her hair and body from several directions. She turned slowly, raising arms, raising legs, craning her neck. Two minutes minimum, you are responsible to make sure you have been thoroughly doused. The liquid streamed down her back, warm but not hot, and sought the path of least resistance through the notch in her backside. She always wondered if anyone was monitoring the wash mode on hidden cameras, but never had the nerve to ask. They would probably lie if they were…

In the drying room, warm air circulated. Brianna placed her hands under the ultraviolet and moved her toes under the lower light display. The rays were imperceptible, they bathed her extremities silently and without feeling. Exit from Level Four was always a pain, but not nearly so arduous as when you had to gain entry into McCabe's lab. By the time you got into your full body positive pressure suit and got your air supply hooked up, you felt as if you had spent half your morning already. The work was interesting but suspicious. Why would you need a three-month security investigation to work on biologics that were contained in the stomach of every person, and why did the University spend so much money on studying and restudying these biologics and their reaction with so many organic compounds, other biologics, enzymes and benign viruses? And why was this Level Four to begin with, where you couldn't bring anything into your workspace, particularly nothing edible? This was a problem for Brianna and her habit of nibbling on five or six small "meals" a day.

The waiver form was even more absurd than the usual waiver at the Bio Lab. Some lawyer must have gotten a hernia just writing it. Still, the pay was great, an extra 20%, and Brianna's student loan, now in its fifth year, was finally getting down to where she did not feel a slave to whatever passed for the system. McCabe was something of a mysterious sort, but pretty relaxed for a senior scientist. She once asked about the value of their work to basic science and was told that remained to be seen. So long as she was paid and had her nights free, unlike other lab jobs where sometimes experiments required round-the-clock monitoring, she was willing to remain and, ultimately, see.

Dried off, she put on one of the disposable robes, moved through the two sets of doors, hearing them click locked behind her, and turned into the women's locker room. Her lips were chapped from the dry air pumped into her mask, and before she dressed she grabbed a small tube of sterile moisturizer and gently massaged the gel around her mouth. The lip cracks hurt briefly but then absorbed the aloe and retreated into mere rough spots. Good thing I don't have a boyfriend at this moment, she thought. Kissing, let alone anything more acrobatic, would be a painful exercise in pleasure.

Brianna walked out of the glass doors to her Toyota SUV. It was an indulgence perhaps, but she had to get to work and the lab was not convenient to public transportation. Driving in New England was a challenge in the winter, and last winter with its hundred inches of snow had convinced her that she needed a four-wheel drive vehicle with good road clearance. It was used and its paint was dulled from five years of being driven in the very conditions it was designed to conquer, but it was reliable, stingy on the gas, and fostered a sense of safety even as other cars were skidding and spinning on hills large and small. The inside smelled like salad and chicken, a combination she kept in the car every workday to satisfy her intense hunger at day's end. Sometimes she would even go through the drill of exiting at lunchtime to rush out and gulp down her snack rather than wait for end-of-shift, although it took her an entire hour to exit, shower, dress, gulp down her meal, and suit up again for reentry.

The lab had not always been so restricted. When the project started, they were at Level One, working at open benches with minimum safeguards. But even then, come to think of it, access was closely controlled, visitors were never allowed unless signed in and known to Dr. McCabe. Then, although Brianna had not noticed any change in the biologics that they were exposing to various enzymes and viruses, suddenly one Monday she showed up to be shuttled to a briefing room for a lecture on Level Four labs. She and the ten other workers spent the rest of that day receiving hands-on training in entry and exit. In a small alcove behind a door which she had not particularly noticed before, at the end of a hallway they never had occasion to use, they were required to practice suiting up and showering off twice, including full rehearsal with nudity, shower, dressing and exiting.

The next surprise was that Tuesday when, reporting into the same alcove, they were shown to an elevator that had a security code and finger-print security access, after which you went down some number of floors (no markings, no floor lights inside) to their new working space, with different locker rooms and another set of showers, double entry doors, and then the lab floor to which all of their work and equipment had been relocated. There also were some additional pieces of equipment, those housed in yet another self-containment room with its own vacuum systems and separate air supply and exhausts. Over time she would observe that on occasion McCabe and Doctor Joseph Creeley, McCabe's principal assistant, carried some double-contained flasks into that room. No one else was ever invited inside. Bob Licatta, Brianna's bench-mate in the lab, began calling him Dr. Creepy and, after a while, the name was adopted by the rest of the junior staff.

Another thing the staff began to notice was that Dr. Creepy was the only person allowed to join McCabe when the guy in the suit would make his frequent periodic visits to the facility. The nameless visitor never did enter the active lab area, however. Bob said he must be afraid of catching some rare disease from the air.

In fact, the time Brianna really began to have some serious concerns, not concerns really but questions, was when she began to notice the frequency with which this visitor, to whom no one was ever introduced, started visiting the lab. A short, powerfully built gentlemen who looked like he was in his forties but clearly could have been a bouncer in the world's worst barroom, moved with crisp precision. Staff agreed that he was, or at least had been, military.

He always retreated to McCabe's outer office beyond the bio-secure zone, always with Dr. Creepy, where they spent a half hour or so, and then he was off again, his high-gloss shoes clicking precisely on the tiled floor. His comings and goings were reported sporadically by staff who happened to be outside the double doors. He never once was seen in a pressure suit.

One night, over beers with the lab workers at The Ball Club, Bob Licatta mentioned that once he had asked McCabe about the visitor, and McCabe had smiled and said that he was a representative of the sponsors of their work and that he hoped, one day, that he might meet and address the lab personnel. The five or six lab techs sitting at their table for their usual Thursday night beers, looked at each other for about two silent seconds, and then everyone laughed at once. "Sure, can't wait," said Bob. "I'm holding my breath," someone else said. Brianna thought yeah…, but did not say a word. Her Sam Adams Summer Ale tasted flat and starchy in her mouth.

6

Simpson went to the hall closet where his regular clothes were hanging, not that he had used them much during his weeks of surveillance. McCabe's periodic reports to someone named Carstons, forwarded to him by Johnston at Langley after apparently being intercepted by the CIA, were uneventful. But intel had concluded that something else was going on aside from basic scientific research.

The house next to McCabe at that point was empty but fully furnished and equipped. No one had yet moved in, no tell-tale evidence of a family going into a new neighborhood. What did that mean? There had been no "for sale" signs, no open houses, no broker peddling the property. Everything about McCabe was being tightly monitored, ever since the CIA intercept from some domestic source to the Russian military suggesting that the lab was a surveillance target and that Dr. McCabe was being "tracked." This unexplainable development was the thing that had led to Simpson's vague assignment in the first place.

Harry Simpson, one of the few senior Black CIA field agents, wasn't cleared to know what was being suspected about the lab, even if indeed his CIA control Heinrich Johnston himself actually knew those details, just that it was "sensitive." He did not need to know. He just needed to keep his eyes open and remember that McCabe was key. He had been hanging around for weeks, securing work as part-time janitor in a nearby building. The lobby of McCabe's lab building was accessible, at least for the two small tenants on the ground floor, a pharmacy and an eyeglass store. Anything beyond the first level was pretty tightly secured.

He had hacked the lab's staff list; the lab's firewall was less than robust when it came to personnel and HR matters. He was able to match up the people, over time, and was particularly interested in one Brianna Flowers, the only person of color working in the most secure area. She was not a party girl, that was for sure. A couple of weeks of light investigation found her mostly at home after work, sometimes at a movie with a female friend. No negative employment record of any kind. Underpaid at that, compared to the men; but no surprise there. A couple of times, he observed Brianna entering The Ball Club, a sports bar a few blocks from her workplace, having a beer with colleagues.

Simpson picked out some gray slacks, loafers, a collared shirt, and decided to pass on a sports coat as the medical nerds in that area seldom bothered, particularly with the advent of warmer weather. He shaved and, for the first time in two weeks, washed his hair. When he went back to his janitorial work tomorrow he would have to grease up his hair beforehand—couldn't afford to look too neat and groomed. Hopefully he could strike up a conversation with Brianna tonight. If she even showed up. She was not a 100% regular on Thursdays, not like some of the others. But the others might be harder to befriend…

The Ball Club was fundamentally nondescript, slick but predictable in Cambridge's bio-tech hub at Kendall Square, where everything was newly built, boxy glass buildings too close to the street to permit the area to be called a neighborhood. A longish bar with the obligatory mirrored wall behind it, punctuated by shelves of liquor, mostly in the lower price range. Simpson sat in the middle of the bar; he had gotten there early. If the lab crowd came in they might be at one end or the other, so the middle was a decent bet. He ordered a beer and caught his reflection— middle-aged Black man neatly dressed, trim, face lined but not too badly. It would be better for this moment if I were ten years younger, he thought; actually, better for all moments. But you have to work with the face you own regardless of what you are trying to achieve through stealth. You do not have much of a choice. Disguises work in the movies, not in the real world.

Wooden tables seating six filled the place from near the front door to the back, where there were a couple of old-fashioned pinball machines and doors to the restrooms and kitchen. On the walls were pennants, and pictures of Boston sports teams from various illustrious eras, smiling Bobby Orr, smiling Carleton Fisk, smiling Tom Brady, smiling Larry Bird, dour Bill Russell. Only Black face on the wall, Simpson thought. And he's scowling. Welcome to The Ball Club.

At a little after five, small groups began to leak in, and about 5:15 a few people from the lab arrived. He knew their faces from the files he had hacked. No Brianna. Beers all around. All around again. Popcorn, finally a plate of greasy nachos. By six it looked like the party would start to break up, without Brianna. Simpson was now nursing his second Yuengling which was warm and full of backsplash. He had to piss. It was hot and noisy and he was standing out like nobody's business, the only solo person in the bar and one of only three people of color (if you ignored the numerous Asians most of whom had stethoscopes draped decorously around their necks). He was getting squeezed by a group of engineers on his right, a couple of bald guys writing formulae on napkins to his left, and at the far end, at the first table, six people from the lab.

Then Brianna walked in briskly, as if on some unseen cue, flustered and a bit breathless. He could only hear snippets: "caught on a problem," "McCabe," "Doctor Creepy" (who the hell was that?). Someone flagged the bartender for a beer, and someone stood up from a stool and let Brianna plop down heavily next to the table. But then a couple of people pretended to look at their watches and began their polite exit dance. A good development, it would be hard to break into so large a group, not that Simpson had much of a plan anyway.

Then the two remaining men left, so that the group now consisted of three females. Was that easier or harder? They really don't train us for this moment, he thought. He was thrown back to his own experience, which is to say unsure embarrassment. Well, he had an investment in the situation, worst that would happen is he'd fail.

"Excuse me. Mind if I join you?"

Polite silence.

"I just moved to Cambridge. From Chicago. I'm Barry Thompson."

Pause again.

"I work for Unitester, in security," he tried. Unitester was a national company conducting lab experiment supervision, with a small office in the building he served as part-time janitor. He mentally crossed his fingers and asked, "You know any of the folks over there?"

Three quick shrugs, and then one of the women introduced herself. Brianna said it was always a good thing to have some friends in a new city, and so he should have a seat. Where was he living? What exactly was security for a company like? What was that again, Unitester? He was, with only a moment of rough sledding, "in" the conversation, easy peasy and a smooth skate from here on. He ordered a round of beers on his tab. He drove thoughts of anything out of his mind except to relax, be whatever was left of himself, get natural. Time enough later for, well, for the job.

He ended the evening with Brianna's home phone number on a napkin in his trouser pocket. He did not mention to her that he already had that number handy, in his computer—along with just about every other item of information about her in the known universe.

7

McCabe carefully separated the egg yolks from four extra-large brown eggs by opening each into his palm, allowing the clear liquid to slip through his slightly spread fingers into the mixing bowl below, and then tossing the shell and yolk into the sink. He took care to intercept any shards of broken shell before they sank into the bottom of the bowl. He had not had time to let the eggs come to room temperature, which would have made the liquid flow more evenly, not to mention alleviate the gentle ache in his palm from the almost-freezing eggs as he laboriously captured the whites for his omelet.

Into the bowl, ever the precise scientist, he then dropped one shake of salt, a half-capful of vanilla extract, a small shot of half-and-half, and just a pinch of sugar to cut the bitterness of the vanilla. After a vigorous mix he quickly poured the eggs into his preheated no-stick skillet, which he had previously sprayed with a butter-flavored non-stick lubricant.

Lowering the gas flame until nearly extinguished, McCabe carefully tilted the frying pan in all directions, making sure the eggs filled the entire circular cooking surface and formed a thin base for his omelet. He did not cover the eggs. He had perfected a rather high flip of the omelet in the air once it had congealed on the bottom surface, and once flipped the former top side would cook soon enough. You had to be careful on both sides of the omelet, the sugar was useful but could create an unwanted char if overheated.

His omelet filling had been slightly preheated in the microwave, not hot but to take the chill off the diced peppers, onions, tomatoes, avocados, just a hint of finely cut kale. He did not sauté the filling, preferring a crispier texture for his interior. At the precise correct moment, he scooped the filling into the middle of his omelet, using his fingers. No sense dirtying extra equipment if you could help it. Not like in the lab, he thought. In the lab, every instrument had a precise function and besides, the scale at which he was working in the lab did not permit the use of fingers even if you could ignore the bacteria those fingers might add to the experiment and, come to think of it, getting that experimental material directly onto one's body was a really really bad idea. Then, with the arrival of Level Four security, the concept of an ungloved hand became an impossibility.

His attention snapped back to his fry pan. Time to use the non-scratching spatula to quickly and evenly fold one half of the omelet over the other half, trapping the filling inside. Always left to right; McCabe was left-handed. And then check to make sure the heat is as low as possible, cover the entire pan and count to fifty at a rapid pace. Prior experiments had demonstrated that fifty was the best count to get a blended taste at an even temperature.

A quick slide off the side of the slippery fry pan onto a large dinner platter, off to the table with knife and fork, coffee already cooling at his seat. Excellent omelet, as always. Coffee cooled enough to drink. The *Globe* opened to the comics. You had to start the day with the comics, you needed fortitude to read the front page and, more difficult still, some of the inner pages. The *Globe* often put the soft stuff on the front page, not quite tabloid style but in a bow to what moved newspapers off the counters of convenience stores and the few remaining actual newsstands.

And better also not to think too far ahead about the lab; time enough to focus on that. Today was an important day, he thought; today his most recent "product," the one he had been targeting for a couple of years, might be ripe for "the test." He certainly had hoped so. In Carstons' last few visits, McCabe had sensed a certain edge, not quite an anger but a hint of frustration. Certainly you did not want to disappoint or frustrate your funding source.

Dishes in the sink, run water in them (cold so the egg residue does not stick), a quick trip upstairs to kiss his still-sleeping bride, and then out to the car for his ride to the lab. He had no briefcase. You did not take information out of the lab.

Opening the door to his Chevy, McCabe glanced next door at number Sixteen. It had been about two weeks since a car began appearing in the driveway, and his wife had mentioned seeing a middle-aged man emerge on a couple of occasions.

He could not see or sense Ivan/Lyle, looking at him from the undisturbed edge of the den venetian blind, as Ivan did most mornings. Ivan sighed. He was bored. McCabe's observed life was boring. What was going on in the laboratory that made Washington, and thus Moscow, so obsessed with the secrecy of the place? Although his mission was not necessarily to learn about the details of the experiments themselves, or whatever else was being developed there. His job was to assess security and look for—well, look for anything that did not feel quite right. Hard to define, but Ivan in the past had some success in feeling that annoying twitch of mind when things did not feel quite right.

8

McCabe never could get used to the newer lab suits. They were lighter and movement was easier, for sure. And the flow of air was constant and cool. Perspiration used to accumulate on his brow, trickle down to his bushy eyebrows, travel downward to the lower corners of his eyes, and dribble down his cheeks in a ticklish random romp. Some of the salty flow would end up in the corners of his mouth, suggesting pretzels and thirst. His armpits and the inside of his arms used to get clammy and his athletes' foot always seemed to flare up as perspiration popped up in his crevices. Most annoyingly, his underwear always ended up with a vertical brown stain running from the top of his rump down to the back of his testicles.

The new suits alleviated all of these discomforts to greater or lesser degree. So why was he so uneasy wearing them? He did not want to identify the reason, but at some level he knew the reason: they were so thin that he was fearful of puncture.

This unspecified sense of fear had not much mattered early on, but today was perhaps different. He had suited up, checked himself by the checklist, and then had Brianna look him over and rerun his checklist, an unusual sequence that made her less talkative and caused her to re-run her own checklist before entering the first door. He did not offer a reason for his caution, and she did not ask.

His arms reached onto the robotics as he called up the microscopic imaging. There they were, innocuous to the eye and a bit too small to analyze. He pushed the button to increase magnification and scan the culture, searching for the theoretically predicted reaction which he had been looking to create, for the tell-tale pinkish hue in the stain which would be the conclusive evidence. He had never had a false alarm, as nothing before ever looked even promising. And visible attributes were only the first step. Without some way to predict likelihood, he would be doing animal testing forever, in the blind, random shots at a tiny target which might not even exist.

All he needed were a few cells. He could culture those cells, he was sure, but he needed a starting point. Clearly the chemical steps and irradiation would not affect all cells in an area, not even a majority. But perhaps a few? Would they be enough?

His back hurt and his eyes were beginning to sting from the air flow. He asked Brianna, through the microphone, to come to the microscope table and spell him for a while. You didn't stand up from this work for a coffee break, not even a water tube was provided in the suits. You didn't open your hood and light up a cigarette or read a few blogs to clear your head. All you could do was get up, take a few steps, stretch yourself to some degree inside your suit, twist your neck until you felt the small bones grind and pop slightly. You were admonished not to undertake any large muscle stretches. The suits no doubt had the flexibility but if you got a large muscle cramp you were a good half hour away from being able to exit, cleanse, and then address the soreness.

Brianna had in front of her a chart listing various possible reactions and their likely effect on the cultures. She was not sure what each might signify, nor whether they were indicative of the desired result or definitive. Indeed, whether the chart's contents were merely theoretical, or if some or all live cells would react in the same way, or any particular way. That—not really understanding the end game—had been the increasingly uncomfortable aspect to the work.

Normally you were looking for a particular thing to have a specific effect, to treat a particular indication or symptom. But with this spate of experiments, neither the exact nature of the transformative process nor the actual application of any of the identified results were articulated. In that sense, Brianna sometimes felt that she had been demoted to a mere maid, cleaning up messes and setting up other peoples' lab tables according to a system she did not understand. And it had been what, six or seven months? Well past the time that McCabe's explanation, that they were doing a pure speculative dive into the as-yet-unexplored resistance of certain strains of common bacteria to chemical or physical stressors or rare enzyme cocktails, any longer made any sense. At least, based on what she knew of the field. Of course, she had only two years of community college and, although she had graduated at the top of her class, McCabe was a full professor with a wall full of awards and a few statuettes in his office—palpable proof that he knew important things that were beyond her ken.

Her mind had wandered. She pulled back samples 884

and 883. She lacked confidence that she had carefully viewed them, even though the computer, tied to the microscope and programmed to highlight those certain indications, had not itself buzzed and halted, its metallic bbbbbbbbbbrr-rrrrrrrinnnngggggggg mocking the failure of the human, its subtext saying "well you screwed up, you are inferior but I bailed out your ass and just maybe you can retain your miserable job a little longer."

McCabe's voice jolted her for no good reason. "I'll take it back for a bit, Brianna. I know it is tedious and duplicative." Ever polite and non-aggressive, a good boss, a very good boss, if you just ignored that he did not tell you what the hell you were really doing.

Afternoon heralded itself with a slight kick-back in McCabe's upper stomach. He had expected that the omelet would have found itself much further south by this time. He had used very tame peppers and onions, not the virulent kinds he preferred, just to avoid this feeling that he could not do anything about. There were no antacids in his suit, no way to ingest them. He had learned to have only one cup of coffee before suiting up, and to strain to void himself beforehand, a task not so easy at his age. He ate his large meal immediately after he unsuited each day, so that his bowels had maximum chance to empty before the next morning. He never ate after 6 p.m. on the day before he was planning to be in the lab. And lately he had planned to be in the lab just about every day. Caused havoc in the family but everyone claimed that they understood.

The wall clock said it was 2 p.m., too early to stop, and he was disappointed with the batches he had screened so far, particularly when he had such high hopes for the day. There is always that irrational belief that if you stop at sample

10,000, then the jackpot is next at 10,001, a belief without logical support but a driver of intense human behavior whether you were talking about slot machine parlors or the laboratory. Well, it was summer, regular quitting time was 4:30 but perhaps he would fix an arbitrary stop today at 4:00. Get home a little early, maybe even take tomorrow off, and then come back and re-cook the remaining petri dishes. He had a couple of chemically modified enzymes he had been thinking about…

The modern electron microscope does not have those tiny little eyepieces you might remember from your own laboratory courses while still at University. It has a real screen, no need to bend over and move your head to make sure you are seeing the whole field. And of course McCabe had the computer reader attached so it was not even clear what your own human role was in the process. Those computer enhancements were very, very expensive. Brianna had thought that whatever was going on must be pretty important because (aside from the institution of super-sterile procedures) the arrival of that computer, and a lot of other specialized equipment she had theretofore only read about, had been casually installed in her lab. She happened to be back on the screen when sample 920 seemed a bit strange to her. She was reaching for the alert button so she could take a closer look when she and McCabe nearly jumped out of their clean suits as the buzzer sounded loud and insistently in the stillness of the late afternoon.

Simpson was showering for his date. Susannah McCabe was seated in her kitchen reading a novella set in Paris in the 19th century. Lyle James Vincent was in his basement, doing 100 push-ups and thinking about the coming hour on his running machine. Sam Harding was at his desk, writing a contract for sewage plant inspections.

Brianna and McCabe were standing next to each other, their suits actually touching from waist to shoulder, their plastic masked faces leaning unnecessarily close to a twelve-inch computer screen, their eyes scanning left and right at a series of odd-shaped squiggles. The buzzer continued its monotone. Brianna and McCabe were too busy to turn it off. The techs outside the lab, looking at their own television monitors showing the whole inside lab space, stood transfixed, not knowing why the buzzer was still ringing, thankful that at least it was not the sirens signaling a bio breach.

In his office on Michigan Avenue in Washington, D.C., Carstons was preparing for his meeting the following morning with General Strykopolos. His assistant knocked, came through the door and handed Carstons a piece of note paper. It contained one sentence: "The buzzer just went off."

9

Strykopolos rolled his shoulders forward and back—
tension always settled there and made the back of his skull
ache. That ache seemed, psychologically, to be exacerbated
by his memory of his brimmed hats, the ones with the
stars on it. He had preferred no headgear, or at worst the
soft beret of special forces, but that seemed so long ago.
His headache certainly hadn't been improved by Carstons'
report, which he tossed dismissively on his desk. He had
not understood much of its contents.

"What the fuck, exactly, are you trying to tell me, Carstons?"
he asked, eyes two black tiny BBs of suspicion set in his
spare face.

Carstons was used to this rush to the bottom line. The
General was primordial in approach, more likely to jump
out of an airplane with a knife in his teeth than listen to
any explanation of more than two sentences. Strykoplos'
looks might be deceiving; wiry rather than muscular, his
pasty narrow face with forehead creases marched upwards
towards his alarming bald spot rimmed with scraggles of
white hair. Seemingly too young to belong to a gung-ho

senior military man, he wasn't very tall and he walked with something of a forward tilt that looked almost like a listing ship. The new military meets the old military, Carstons thought, but kept that to himself.

"General, it's simple if we skip the whole first section on the science. In a nutshell, there are certain organisms, bacteria if you will, that occur naturally within the body—the digestive tract of virtually every human being, everywhere on earth. Doesn't matter if they are in New York or Tokyo. Doesn't matter if they are in Moscow or Baghdad or Beijing. Everybody's got 'em. You and me, as we sit here, we've got 'em."

"And they don't hurt us, not at all. Seems not even if someone has an immune system deficiency. No one is sure exactly what all of them do, if anything, but they are benign."

Strykolopos shifted in his chair. He thought Carstons was a pompous asshole. He was however, a pompous asshole who held the ear of that pompous asshole of a Congressman who, in turn, happened to control the U.S. military budget appropriations. And the General did not take that fact lightly because if Congress screwed with the military budget then the Army, indeed the whole country not to mention the whole world, got screwed. Strykolopos could handle the President all right, she didn't know shit from shinola and relied heavily on his counsel. But Congress was not so easy to manipulate. In a time of perceived loss of American hegemony and increased Chinese military adventures in the South China Sea, not to mention the meaningless mélange of Middle East murder and those nuts in North Korea, who needed confusion at home? "Yeah, right, got it," he offered.

Carstons did not mind being patronized. He had little

ego at the start of his public service, and he found that even that much was an impediment. Without the killer instinct, he had early realized that he best served as one of the really smart pilot fish swimming below the shark's body, important to the ecosystem but without personal armament. He had to stay out of the way of the shark's jaws but, if he did, none of the other big fish would mess with him. He knew that Congress, and others in the government in past years, had understood how Carstons swam: never a threat, willing to do any task regardless of anything else, and without enough ego left even to be tempted to turn in a different direction.

"So there is this clear, odorless, tasteless concentrated liquid that McCabe was working on. He thinks he has finally found it, a formula to make it." Carstons paused. How to explain the effect of this liquid to someone who saw all of science as a weapons system? "It alters these natural biologics in someone's body. All you have to do is drink it. It affects these bacteria. It changes their properties. It makes it invisible to the body's defenses and it multiplies and kills."

"Kills what?"

"Once swallowed it gets into the blood and kills everything the infected blood touches. The stomach, the arteries, the heart, the lungs. It kills the organism. It is not itself contagious by air or touch, not like the flu or anything like that. So it is very, very hard to diagnose, to discover. And the change in these organisms under a microscope apparently is so subtle that it may well avoid detection. It kills fast, also. And we think painlessly. We are going to work with some animals on that part."

The General leaned forward and almost whispered. "So

this is what, a biological weapon? Are you telling me this is what we usually call 'germ warfare'?"

"Yes, of a certain type." It was important to Carstons to try to position the General's view of this development in a way that was favorable or at least neutral, even if it took a twist of nomenclature. Personally, his view was that germ warfare was just efficient warfare with great ancillary impact and consequently great efficacy, and if you had such a tool that would not spread between people and would thus protect the protagonist, it seemed like a pretty neat development. Germs, bombs, bullets all killed. The moral distinction was non-existent, as was indeed (if you pushed him for his view) the moral scale of values itself.

The General was not a wholly insensitive man. No conclusion should be derived from this narrative, none is intended or implied. "You are no doubt aware, Mr. Carstons, that there are treaties about this sort of thing, yes? In that context, how might I explain all this to our President?" It was a question, but not a question the gravity of which was contained in the words utilized, but rather implicit in the unspoken, unspeakable answer.

"We are looking into that. What we've signed. Whether this is within the ambit of what we signed." Carstons looked down not because he was ashamed of his answer, just that he was nonplused not to have yet received definitive instructions on the matter.

"What do you want the Joint Chiefs to do about this now? Or me, what do you want of me? Why are we having this conversation today? I expect you do not want me to share this with the President, at least at this juncture? I presume this is pretty top secret, yes?" The General's eyebrows raised, deepening the horizontals on his forehead, creating violent crevices of taut flesh, threatening to flow upwards onto his nearly bald scalp and furrow his entire body from his neck up.

Why indeed? Carstons did not want to share his view as to the "why." Not yet. And he needed more information from McCabe: things like cost, transportation, requisite density, specific speed of reaction at different concentrations, ability to prevent reverse engineering.

"Just a heads up," Carstons said, gathering his few papers and preparing to stand up. He looked up over his wire rims, head lowered for emphasis. "The Congressman asked me to be sure you were personally alerted to all of this."

"Huh," said the General.

10

A week before Simpson was found swimming face down in the pond, McCabe and Carstons met in Boston's North End on a Monday night, when they could find a quiet back table in one of the coffee shops lining Hanover Street. Carstons had suggested that he stop visiting the lab, but they had to talk. McCabe was trying to dunk the thick end of a biscotti into an intensely black and tiny espresso cup when Carstons sat down at his table, dressed in khakis and a knit shirt and loafers with no socks.

"You look like a college professor," McCabe observed.

"And you look like someone with no sense of spatial relations. Can't you see that you cannot jam that cookie into that teacup?"

"It's not a cookie," McCabe said with a half sigh. He did not like being out in Boston at night when he could be home, helping one of his sons with his calculus or watching his television programs. The high drama of an off-site meeting struck him as over-the-top to the point of paranoia.

Carstons let it pass. "I need your assessment about

certain attributes of your invention. What about density? To be effective, how much would I have to drop into, say Quabbin Reservoir? And is it stable if I carry it? Can I put it into any kind of container, or do you need glass or something like that? What effect does temperature have on it? What sort of volume can you produce if we, well, let's say if we 'gear up?' That sort of thing."

The waiter came over, his white apron splotched with coffee stains, looking down at Carstons, waiting for his order. "Uh, double espresso, and a cannoli. You have cannoli?"

The waiter rolled his eyes for effect. "Yeah, maybe. You want whipped cream? Ricotta? You want regular or chocolate chip? You want minis or big ones? How many ya want?"

Carstons smiled thinly with a smile that was not really a smile. "How about one large with ricotta. And a double. Can you do that?"

The waiter narrowed his eyes, he did not like this guy, smug little bastard. And what's with no socks, the guy has to be 55 if he's a day. Well, takes all kinds. "Comin' up," he said.

McCabe used the moment to think of the right answer. There were pure science advantages, insights from his work at the lab, but then again he doubted that Carstons' people, whomever they were (the money came by wire transfer to the account, no details about the sender), had a purely scientific focus. He had been assured that Carstons was affiliated with the government, that is McCabe's own government, but beyond that the silence spoke loudly.

"Still working all of that out," he said. "But a few things are pretty clear. The agent is stable, can be transported in anything clean and dry that holds liquid, is immune to temperature within normal human range. Not sure how long it lasts but at least a few weeks; likely much longer given what we suspect. It multiplies itself to a point, after which it must necessarily degrade, at a rate we do not know. If it mixes with saline solutions, it falls apart quickly so in the ocean, for example, it is ineffective. As to quantities? That's just a matter of money." He looked up at Carstons. "That's not a problem for you, is it? I mean if you needed an oil truck full of the stuff and I told you I needed two months and ten million dollars, you would just say 'uh-huh,' wouldn't you?"

"What are you frosted about, Caleb? Haven't we always treated you right?"

"Yeah but you know why I'm a little weirded out here. Don't try to finesse me at this point of our, well, relationship."

Carstons from his vantage point was not surprised at McCabe's reaction. It would be only natural. Not the first scientist to invent something for the thrill and challenge of it and then have second thoughts. Best to let that pass also. He pretended to cool his espresso, which arrived with what he was sure was a purposeful spill of a little coffee into his saucer.

"Look," Carstons said. "Let's not screw around here. Neither of us fell off the back end of that turnip truck. Just tell me what you know."

Caleb took the matter-of-fact inquiry as absolution. He was already in the water, he now had to swim a little, no sweat.

"A thimble-full handles 100 gallons. At least initially.

That is because when you put it in plain water there is a reaction that drives multiplication. Efficacy of course has to do with how long before someone drinks it. If you drink it right away you need more. If you wait a couple of weeks, the concentration has increased and you need less. There is some endpoint we have not yet calculated. There is likely a minimum ingestion required, and likely a time when the agent becomes, well, stale or wears down, but we don't know that with precision." Caleb paused. He swallowed and blinked. "Would know a lot more if we had some primates to work with," he ventured.

Carstons sipped. The espresso was bitter, pungent, the smell filled his nostrils and coaxed drops of sweat under his nose.

"People you mean?"

"No, no. Not people. Whoa, what the hell are you suggesting? Are you nuts? Monkeys. Several types, I can identify them genetically when the time comes. But maybe a couple of hundred." He gulped again and lowered his voice to a whisper. "Might need a special facility, the places around Cambridge that handle animals aren't really set up for—well for what is likely to be the results of our testing." Caleb thought, this is worse than I thought, and I did not have great expectations to start with.

They were hard to see through the front window. The car lights and the glare from restaurants danced across the glass, alternately obscuring everything inside and turning the windows into imperfect mirrors. Lyle was not used to seeing Caleb get on the subway rather than get into his car at the end of the day and had decided to follow him. He lit a large cigar and leaned against the wall of a building across the street from the café. It was hard to be inconspicuous. Halfway through he got nervous, snubbed his cigar underfoot and drifted onto a line waiting entry into an Italian bakery, still keeping his eye on the café door.

If Lyle was having trouble feeling invisible, Simpson had an even harder time. Not a lot of Black guys leaning on buildings in the Italian district. He had figured out Lyle's routine by simply following him from his home a few times, but had not really speculated on the range of possibilities until he had focused on Lyle as the new equation in Caleb McCabe's life. Sure enough, here was Lyle watching McCabe meeting with someone whom Simpson needed to identify pretty quickly. He knew enough from Brianna to know that something was going on at the lab beyond the usual academic meandering, and he had seen the man now with McCabe enter the lab building a couple of times dressed in a suit. He knew that much.

But Simpson did not know how Ivan/Lyle fit into the picture, nor who Carstons was, nor exactly what was happening in the lab, even though he had been dispatched by his people to figure out the ultimate disposition of all those cash transfers the Agency has accidentally found buried in a discretionary military account.

There was another thing Simpson did not know. He did not know that as Lyle had turned quickly to enter the bakery, he had seen Simpson across the street, a Black face in a flow of white faces, and recognized him as someone who had walked by Lyle's new house a couple of times, a conspicuous presence in lily-white Newton.

And what Lyle did not know was whether the Black guy was following McCabe to protect him or for some other purpose. Or, come to think of it, whether the Black guy was following him.

Carstons stepped through the door alone and walked back towards downtown. Lyle let him go. He would stay with McCabe and in any event he did not want to jump out into the street just then. He did see Simpson fall in behind Carstons, which meant that the Black guy likely was not working for Carstons. But that still left a lot of possible employers.

Ten minutes later Caleb emerged with a white box tied with string, no doubt full of Italian pastries, and started walking back to the subway. Had to be going home to Susannah with a peace offering of sweets, Lyle thought. Might as well sit and finish his own coffee and cheesecake. One thing for sure, the Italian bakeries in Boston really saturated their products with lots of sugar.

11

A few days after his North End meeting with Carstons, and several days before Simpson turned up dead, McCabe took two trains and an Uber to wend his way to South Station. Then he sat in South Station nursing an iced coffee for almost two hours, reading his novel, and looking carefully at everyone around him or walking past him. Truth be told, McCabe only got through about fifteen pages and, when he next picked up his book, he had no recollection of what those pages contained.

At lunchtime he walked to Federal Street, passed through building security with his driver's license, and presented himself at thirtieth floor reception for the sandwich lunch he had scheduled with Sam Harding.

"Thanks so much," Caleb said, as Harding passed him his tuna on rye, no lettuce, two pickles.

"It's only a sandwich," Harding said.

"No, I meant for meeting with me on short notice."

"No worries, Caleb. But you have to tell me why the mystery. Are you looking for a lawyer professionally? Is this about the neighborhood, is it personal?"

"I don't know if I need a lawyer. Not sure what I need. Except maybe my head examined. I mean, what I tell you, it's all confidential, right? Do I have to pay you something…?" He trailed off, fingering his sandwich, squeezing it tightly, small globs of tuna fish soaked in mayonnaise dropping onto his paper plate.

"No, no, not what I was getting at. Glad to just chat with you. Whatever you tell me is confidential even if you never ever hire me." The panic did not fade from McCabe's face, almost scary if not comedic. "Just relax, eat, talk, whatever."

"Well, I want to tell you a story. Something I am not really allowed to tell you. At least not a lot of it. But my life has gotten very weird lately." He chomped into the middle of his sandwich half, took a couple of quick chaws, and started talking.

"So, I am a professor at Harvard but I also work at a laboratory that is supported by, well, outside funding. Over in Cambridge, near MIT actually. My specialty is dealing with viruses, proteins, biologics, and the effect of enzymes on them. Effects on the genetic expression of proteins. Modifying organic molecules by exposing them to varied stimuli for medical purposes, research, treatment."

Armed with having read a recent article in the *Wall Street Journal*, I assured him I knew what he was talking about. "Oh, sure, genetic modification. You mess with the genes, right?"

"Not really. There are many other ways, not completely understood, to affect large molecules and viruses. At least theoretically. Very hard to predict. We use chemicals, actually; proteins, enzymes, we deal with covalent attachments.

Affects infectivity." He paused and looked up expectantly for me to acknowledge him. I gave a quick little nod and poked at my cobb salad, appropriately abashed at having failed to guess what the man's life work involved.

"Well, that part really isn't what I wanted to tell you. Forgive me. It will only take about an hour, I know you are busy…"

So we talked until my secretary left at 5:30, and we talked after I called home to say I was caught at the office working late, and we talked after we went to the vending machines for a couple of candy bars which we washed down with some Johnny Walker Blue I kept in my credenza. Nothing but the best for my clients.

"And there's one last thing," he said, finally pulling down his tie and undoing his top button.

"Jesus, Caleb, what you have just told me is more than enough, talking to that government agent and all." I had decided not to complicate McCabe's fears by sharing with him my own encounters with the CIA.

"Yes, well, it isn't everything. Now this is really going to sound nuts, but I am sure I am being followed."

I held my breath a beat. It truly sounded nuts. Is this guy really a paranoid head case who has wasted half a day and half a night?

"Followed?" I managed to croak.

"Yes. Sure of it. At least one guy, he moved into the house immediately next door. Keeps to himself. Single man. Really in shape. But I have seen him around the lab three or four times, just walking through the lobby. No reason for him to be there, doesn't work there. Pretty sure doesn't work nearby, either. And then, the night at the café I told you about when I met with the guy who controls our funding? I think I saw this neighbor. And, this is really crazy, there is this guy who I think is a janitor in our building, maybe next door actually? He sort of stands out, he is a very dark Black man. He always seems to be out on the street when I am going to lunch or going home. I swear I saw him that night also. What the hell was that all about?" Caleb was all worked up, sweating again but face pale and pasty, punctuated by an occasional red splotch, his mustache seemed cemented flat to his upper lip. He took a dirty handkerchief from his trousers and ran it over his face to sop up the moisture.

"Shit," he said, his voice falling to a wistful sigh. "What am I going to do?"

Then he looked up. After about eight hours of talking, he was not just making a generally depressive, confused exclamation. He actually expected me to tell him what he should do.

In my business, I make it a point to not answer questions when I am totally out of my depth, not a discipline for which most lawyers are noted I might add. The truth is always better; I never have been smart enough to remember what I invent on the spot.

"I don't know. I don't think there is a playbook for this. But there has to be a bunch of options. I would like to think about those options. I really don't think you should do anything tomorrow, just as a reaction, ya know?"

"I know that but I am running out of time. I actually have all the answers they are looking for. Some others in the lab know many of them. If this guy starts poking around, he is going to find out I am stalling. This is serious stuff, government stuff. Military stuff. Deadly things, ya know? This guy asked me very specific questions. They made sense only if someone was going to use this as a weapon." McCabe paused, then continued.

"I'm no hero but I don't think I can do what they want me to do. I'm scared to death but, if I talk to someone who might be able to help me, I mean that could be the very place, the very person who sent me the money and who employs this—guy, this very guy."

Sometimes acknowledging that you are in a corner clarifies where you are and makes you calmer, more accepting. I didn't know McCabe well enough to know how he would react, but he clearly was going to have some sleepless nights at the very least. Might as well tell him the obvious so it's out there for him.

"You took the first step, you asked for help. Now you have to take the advice you were looking for. Go home. Have another drink. Go to sleep. Tomorrow is Saturday. Let's talk again around noontime." A couple of bad thoughts came over me. "Not by phone. Take a walk by my house— be there at 12:30. I will be outside doing something. We'll chat. I'll invite you in for a soda or a beer. Just natural, just like that. Meanwhile say hello to Susannah for me." I rethought that one real fast. "On second thought," I said softly, "at this point you better not."

12

A few weeks before Simpson ended up in the water, he finally got Brianna Flowers to his apartment which was, of course, fully wired. After a little too much wine and a prim but satisfying visit to the bedroom, Simpson propped himself up in bed and raised with Brianna her concern for her own safety in the lab, which concern of course did not exist. But as Simpson rightly guessed, would lead to a conversation about her other worries at the laboratory. While he had been sifting through the personality issues, Simpson had also picked up enough information about the science and the level of bio security to make him very interested.

According to Brianna, Caleb was a good boss but pretty nervous. Dr. Creepy was, well, creepy. The periodic, suited visitor, middle-aged and vaguely military in bearing, who never came inside the secure doors but visited regularly both with McCabe and Dr. Creeley had been described to him, and Simpson made a mental note to consider if this was the same fellow he had observed in the North End the prior week. In mock innocence, Simpson asked Brianna why she didn't just sit Caleb down and tell him everything she was thinking and ask him to respond. Just before she dozed off, Brianna shook her head slowly as it drooped towards the pillow. When she woke up, that still would not seem to be such a great idea.

The next morning, at about the same time as Brianna gathered her things to be gently and decorously ushered out of Simpson's cramped quarters, Heinrich Johnston sat in his CIA conference room in Virginia replaying Brianna's recorded rambling list of work complaints, taped in Simpson's bedroom. His suspicions about the laboratory seemed to be justified, that was for sure. Johnston was feeling pretty lucky to have assigned Simpson, also; not sure many other agents would have had the brains, or the fortuitous pigmentation, to get Brianna to shine a light into the laboratory and its suspected secrets. And he was pretty sure that the periodic visitor to the lab also was with the government but was unknown to him and (he presumed) to the Agency.

There might be things that Johnston was still not privy to, but given his specifically designated assignment to McCabe's case, it was just about inconceivable that his superiors were holding back any information they actually possessed. Indeed, their lust to learn what was going on was itself evidence that they were clueless.

Lyle was only slightly surprised to see Brianna exit Simpson's apartment building. He had decided the prior night to follow Brianna when she left the bar with a Black man who might have been the person he had seen outside the café in the North End, and when she had ended up spending the night he surmised that Simpson was not just a workman hanging around. That was possible, but Lyle had a great sense of smell for things that were odorous of professional involvement. He was tired, deadly tired, having closed the coffee shop at 1 a.m. and having walked around for over four hours until Brianna exited, but he knew she was going home and then to the laboratory. Where was the Black man going?

A couple of hours later Simpson emerged, dressed in work overalls and with a Red Sox baseball cap on his head. He took the MBTA to the Kendall Square station and walked briskly into the building across the street from McCabe's laboratory. About 8:30 McCabe bustled into his building, followed ten minutes later by Brianna Flowers. Shortly after that, the Black man started pulling green plastic barrels to the curb from the alley next to his building, just the way a good janitor should. Lyle had learned how a lot of pieces fit together that night, but he had been awake now for almost thirty hours and was tired as hell. He jumped on the Green Line subway, walked to his house and went to sleep in the living room with his shoes still on his feet.

13

"I have an appointment with a Dr. McCabe," the man said rather importantly to the pudgy guy in the security company uniform at the front desk. Khaki pants, shirt open at the neck and pulling at the buttons across his stomach, flabby and in his fifties, no weapon; some security officer. I could take him in a heartbeat, the visitor thought, before this piece of beef could ever even think to push whatever security warning button there might be in a drawer or in the desk well or on the small counter with a few archaic toggles.

"Your name?"

"Nash Berenson. *Cambridge Chronicle*."

The guard picked up the clipboard and flipped a page. "Oh, yeah, here you are." He passed the clipboard over the desk, a felt tip pen connected by a white string to the board by a sloppy knot tied through the hole of the top clasp.

"Sign next to your name, please. And put in the time —it's, call it 10 a.m."

The guard must have pushed some buzzer because a

slight young woman in scrubs came down the hallway from the right, gave him a flash of a half-smile, and waved her hand as she turned back down the hall, inviting him to follow. He fingered the business card he had in his left jacket pocket, printed in Boston (he had bought 100 of them to just get one that he needed), bearing the name of a reporter whose by-line he had seen in the newspaper.

He was shown into a closed room, no windows, a metal table and four chairs. "Please wait here," said the woman, and left him sitting in a hot and stuffy room with nothing to drink.

Dr. Caleb McCabe promptly arrived, hiding pretty well his annoyance at having to do an interview with the press, let alone the *Cambridge Chronicle*, a thin weekly consisting mostly of ads for futons, student furniture, and the performances of ludicrously named post-punk rock bands. But he had learned that if you acted as if you were doing something worrisome, people concluded you were doing something worrisome. Best to behave casually, like real people do.

"We're thinking of doing a column, a weekly on local laboratories. The neighborhood is full of them, all those medical and drug companies, MIT labs, start-ups and all. Lots of our readers, our younger readers, work in them or they pass them on the way to school. The older readers, this is all a mystery, what is happening behind those walls, ya know?" The man paused to give Caleb enough time to nod assent—he did indeed know.

"So frankly yours is, well, about the biggest building around and I thought I'd come here first. Ask you a few questions if you don't mind." He paused for effect and quickly added, "Nothing to pry into your top-secret stuff," with a broad smile and a half snort that carried the message that of course he did not think that anything secret in fact was going on.

"Well, always glad to meet the press so to speak," Caleb lied, and none too convincingly. "If you could go online, I can give you the URL, you can see my specialty at Harvard, the study of biologics and viruses. You know," voice dropped confidentially as if revealing a dark secret, "we do not know a lot about viruses, not a lot at all." Pause of emphasis. "Well, in any event I am interested in those viruses that don't really infect people. What do they do? Can they be useful? So at this lab we are, if you will, looking at some of the very many viruses that exist, seeing how they work. Can we make use of them? Can we see what makes them benign and apply that learning to those viruses which are in fact harmful. Uh—well, that's it really... That sort of thing. Is what we do."

"So that is really interesting," said the man, and in that he was himself not lying. "So Harvard pays for all of this, this lab that isn't even on the campus?"

McCabe was caught short by the question but decided to lie again. "Yes, of course," he said.

"That's interesting, I will be sure to put that in my article," said the man, making notes on his iPad.

"Oh, well, that is really not, you know, not important," said McCabe, who could picture the ramifications if his colleagues on the faculty saw that little misstatement. "I mean, they do but not directly." How to get out of this? "You know, that's off the record," Caleb declared, a slight mist of sweat attacking his forehead.

The reporter smiled. Clearly Harvard was not paying

for this. That was what he wanted to know. There were not that many other possible funding sources either.

"Doctor, let me tell you something about the press. If something is off the record, if it is as we say for background, you have to make that clear before you say it. You cannot go back and fix what you say." Now it was the reporter's turn to pause. "But don't worry, I'm here to write a human-interest story, not make things uncomfortable for our Cambridge neighbors. If you don't want me to mention that, then it's out!"

Good, thought McCabe. "Well, thanks," said McCabe. Dammit, he hated these moments.

"So, Doc, do you think I can take a look at the lab, maybe take a couple of pictures? I can get a photographer here tomorrow morning if that works."

This time McCabe was not going to get trapped. "No photographs please, but I would be happy right now to let you look into the laboratory, through one of the glass windows. You of course cannot go in; viruses you know. I mean we are pretty sure that we know that our viruses are safe, but we can't have visitors coming and going, I am sure you appreciate that." McCabe rose, both to cut off the conversation and to usher his visitor to an internal window a few yards down the hall from the room in which they were talking, where he could see a couple of wash up rooms, two tables with electron microscopes, a refrigerator. The double doors, first floor preliminary Level Four wash-up areas and elevator were around the bend, purposefully not visible from the first viewing window.

The man looked, asked questions, asked if the people he saw in the green and white clothes were all doctors, asked if they were students as some looked so young, asked if the workers came from Cambridge, asked if they were hiring more people, asked if Caleb ever came home with a cold or the flu, rambled a bit, then looked at his watch and shook Caleb's hand and walked out with the same purposeful gait with which he had entered.

Caleb went to the vending machine and punched the button for a strong cup of tea. He had more important things on his mind, not the least of which was his recent meeting with his neighbor the lawyer, and what to tell Carstons when he again called for an update.

On the way out, the reporter left a small cardboard box in the men's room just off the entrance lobby, adhesive holding it in place underneath the lip of the counter adjacent to the bottom of the sink. He walked briskly to Mameleh's delicatessen on Main Street and insisted on a table in back, not at the counter where they tried to stick him. He was halfway through his corned beef and chopped liver sandwich when Lyle sat down silently across from him.

"How'd it go?"

"No worries but no photos." The man slipped the tape cartridge quickly across the table, and Lyle covered it with his palm and dropped it into his pocket.

"And the device?"

"I left it in the men's room near the entrance. Couldn't get deep into the place but everyone's gotta piss sometime, and it's not a time when your sense of security is all that high."

Lyle frowned. "That the best you could do?"

The man stopped in mid-chew. "No, I purposely fucked up and I left the antennae hanging in plain view. Yeah, it was the best I could do in the circumstances." He paused, took another large chomp out of his sandwich, masticated it as quickly as he could, little bits of rye bread adhering to his thin mustache. "Next time, do your own shit. What do you say, I'm an amateur?"

Lyle thought, they sent me someone touchy. Better if I did it myself but how could I, he thought, I'm living next door to the guy. "Well, just an expression, no worries," he said. The man looked down to pick up his pickle, and when he looked up Lyle was gone.

"Shithead," he mumbled to himself. These implanted guys really think their crap don't stink, he thought. Wish I was back in Europe…

14

The McCabes seemed to be preparing for an end-of-summer vacation; their sons were pumping up the bike tires and attaching the bike rack to the rear of the SUV. Susannah was talking to the gardener, who was nodding and pointing. The Thursday *Globe* was not left in the driveway; the Friday milk delivery never arrived. That Friday morning, Caleb did not chug into his office, and shortly thereafter he came outside in cargo shorts, his hairy legs slightly bowed. He had more hair on his calves than on the top of his head, Lyle noticed.

That night, Lyle walked out his door around 10 p.m. smoking a cigarette and took a walk around the block. The lights on the timer in the McCabe living room clicked off around 10:30. The neighborhood around Windwood Circle was quiet, as quiet as—well, as any street in a bedroom suburb at that hour. He walked to his own front door, then turned slowly towards the McCabe house, slipped along the trimmed evergreen bushes, popped the basement door, disabled the alarm control box in the basement before going upstairs where the intrusion sensors were located, and let his eyes slowly adjust to the semi-darkness. Only then did he put on his night vision glasses.

He turned on the lamp on the timer, but did not want to light up the place like a Christmas tree. He slightly opened each venetian blind and opened each drape a few inches to let the streetlight give him some help. McCabe's den was the obvious place to start, but it seemed disappointing at first. The desk was unlocked and just held checkbooks, bills, a couple of files with insurance policies. The checkbooks were not accompanied by bank statements and were not totaled. It was impossible to tell how much McCabe had in ready cash, particularly if there were significant off-line deposits, they would likely be wired to accounts without checkbooks lying around.

Where was the safe? Most people had at least a small safe. A house of this vintage, nice house, pre-war, it might even have a wall safe somewhere. If there were a safe with important information, of course, it might be more sophisticated in terms of its disguise and location, but first things first. He tapped all walls, moved all diplomas, checked behind a large and very bad painting of a golf course, stamped lightly on the floor. Nothing.

He turned to leave the den; perhaps the master bedroom next. He maintained his quiet movements, stepped gently on the rugs, went down the hall, turned to approach the stairway, and found himself face to face with a person who was as surprised as Lyle.

Actually, seemingly more surprised; the person stood there long enough for Lyle to deliver a crisp karate chop to the base of his skull. The person collapsed straight down on the floor, a marionette whose strings all had been cut at once. Grabbing the person's collar, he pulled him across the floor until the light from the living room lamp shed enough glow for him to see what he had gotten.

Simpson lay on the floor, face up, a small trickle of blood leaking from his left nostril. Lyle reached down quickly, ripped the pocket of Simpson's shirt and stuffed it into his nose. No sense getting blood all over the place while he figured out what to do.

It did not take Lyle long to decide that it was a nice evening for Simpson to take a swim.

15

Simpson was born in Hasbrouck Heights, New Jersey. His father was a carpenter. His mother taught kindergarten. He graduated from Rutgers with honors, fenced and swam, and was recruited right out of school, trained for the field, showed intelligence and aptitude and a high pain threshold. He was smart enough to put Brianna and McCabe and something in the lab all together, smart enough to gather lots of data, smart enough be be scared shitless by what he was learning, smart enough to try to get to Harding's house that night of July 22 because there were a lot of cars there and he wanted to know why Doctor Joseph Creeley, affectionately known in the lab as Dr. Creepy, was attending such a late-night meeting.

Not smart enough to know that his ploy to get to Creeley was unartful; not smart enough to realize that Johnston had alerted the Newton police that one of his Black operatives would be knocking around lily-white Newton and they should keep a protective eye out for him; not smart enough to realize that when he went to disable the McCabe burglar alarm and found it disconnected that there might be a problem; not smart enough to act fast when he ran into someone in the middle of the night, wearing night goggles, in a presumably empty house.

Simpson had been on the Rutgers swim team, but when Lyle quietly slipped him into Bullough's Pond just before dawn, when the ebbing moon had just set, his breaststroke just wasn't up to the task. Not a nice night for a swim.

PART TWO

2027

16

Since the police had searched his house, Sam Harding had been quite content to forget all about the incident from 4 years earlier. Whatever the police and Federal Government was after, he concluded that it had nothing to do with him, nor his family. They were innocent tangential players in someone else's drama, not even real victims; just bystanders at a drive-by shooting. Worry about waiting for the next shoe to drop had been replaced by surprise that no one ever contacted him again, followed by the relief of knowing that the powers that be had realized what he knew all along: some guy sat down on his front steps and then someone else made him dead.

And as for Harding's intense office conversation with McCabe about his lab several years ago? When he met with McCabe the following day outside Harding's house, McCabe had decided he had said too much already, and asked Harding to just forget the whole thing. Sam certainly had no interest in sharing all that with Johnston or the police at that time, getting himself yet more deeply mired in things he did not understand.

Some people never seem to change, or they change in such benign ways that the difference is sensed as natural, appropriate, unremarkable. Some people do not gain a gut from beer or inactivity. Some people gray at the temples in an attractive slow creep of silver, never quite going to white, and certainly never quite suffering a moving hairline. Some people stay at ease with themselves, their gait and demeanor a constant; they present the same at 50 as they did at 30. Heinrich Johnston was one of those people.

When Harding sat down on a bench in Post Office Square Park, as he was opening the plastic carton that protected his Chicken Caesar, about to pour the small cup of dressing onto the salad, guilty for using the whole container but then again it was so small and the salad itself was so healthy that he figured the calories balanced out, he concluded to himself that he could still report to his wife that he was continuing to "eat well." As Harding looked up to observe the direction of the early fall wind, to make sure that his salad and dressing were safely oriented, the sight of that familiar face in a dark tight-fitting suit, old-fashioned tab collar, tie in subdued gray, caused a slight jerk of his body. He watched some white gritty dressing dribble onto his charcoal slacks. The stain looked uncomfortably like a bodily discharge.

"Gonna leave an unfortunately located stain," Harding heard himself say out loud as he pulled out his breast handkerchief and began to dab tentatively, unhappy that the hanky linen seemed unwilling to absorb any of the dressing.

"Sorry to startle you," Johnston said.

I busied myself with my stained lap, which allowed me some time to organize a response which was far calmer than my nerves might otherwise have allowed.

"Shit," I said, just to fill the silence and make the point that I was not ignoring Johnston, I was just otherwise importantly engaged.

We sat side by side for a couple of minutes while I finished my housekeeping and mixed the dressing into the greens with a white plastic fork, then speared a thin chicken strip and chewed it suspiciously. The chicken had that moist slick semi-glaze of a piece of poultry best eaten several days ago when, I suspected, it first made its trip into the plastic container. Johnston sat quietly; patience was a virtue and a tool in his line of work. He knew that, sooner or later when I was mentally reset, I would speak first.

"To what do I owe this honor after three years, Agent Johnston?"

"Just a few questions, sir, if you do not mind. Just following up. By the way, it's been almost four years."

"Really. Hadn't focused on that. Frankly haven't been thinking about the whole thing at all. You know, if I did not remember to say something to you years ago when you went through my house, it's not likely my memory is going to be improved over all this time."

"Have you heard lately from your friend Dr. McCabe?" Johnston had the tactical virtue of just ignoring anything that was not moving in the direction that Johnston happened to be moving at the time.

"No, not since they moved away. But you must know that, yes? You guys must know exactly where he is. Some suburb of D.C. in Virginia, yes?"

"He moved a couple of Springs ago. Have you heard from him, spoken to him since then?"

"No, actually. My wife got some change of address note from Susannah I think. We have not seen them, though."

I paused. I did not like Johnston but sensed that my family was no longer in anyone's crosshairs, so what the hell.

"Didn't go to D.C. to see my son. Of course you know he goes to college there, right? And you must know that McCabe and I haven't written or emailed or phoned, you guys have all that watched, right?" I was pleased with my sarcasm, but not with Johnston's response.

"Actually we only had taps and traces at McCabe's end, not on your end anymore, so if he used a device of which we are unaware we might have missed it."

"You tapped my phone? Are you kidding? What the fuck is with you guys?"

"Relax, counsellor, I got the warrant. Nothing to worry about."

"Well you can go straight to hell unless you want to sit here and watch me contact my Congressman. You people are not to be believed!"

I was staring straight at Johnston, using my version of an angry defiant glare, and was thus not prepared for the response.

"McCabe died yesterday in Arlington, Virginia."

The air went out of me. "Oh, that's terrible. Did not know." I paused, looked down, then upwards, all rancor gone. "How did it happen?"

"Officially, he was accidentally killed while riding his bicycle to work."

"Oh, poor Susannah. The kids are a bit older also but... Uh, am I supposed to now ask you what you meant by 'officially'?"

Johnston did not smile. Not just at the moment. He did not smile ever, I surmised.

"We believe he was killed on purpose."

"Noooooo." I heard myself dragging out the word into something like a half-moan.

"Did you ever meet Dr. McCabe's Newton neighbor? A new neighbor, moved in around the time of the Simpson episode?"

"Shit, I should call my wife, she will want to call Susannah." I looked up.

"What did you just say? Sorry..."

"I was wondering if you ever got to know a neighbor of Dr. McCabe, someone who moved in next door. His name was Lyle Vincent. Or that's what he said at the time."

17

The President was more than halfway through her first term and it was beginning to feel like it would be her only term. It was a feeling of disbelief and frustration. She kept getting hung up on the insoluble Middle East and the domestic political game being played around the serious on-the-ground issues.

And the meeting with the Joint Chiefs had not gone well. Her adviser, retired General Gregory Strykopolos, certainly seemed to understand the dynamics of the military, but he also seemed to carry with him some old animosities that ran both ways and which seemed to cloud communications. Today, he particularly seemed to aggravate the Air Force. And there was also a subtext she needed to get underneath, a brief segue into some discussion of weapons delivery that surfaced and then seemed to submerge from consideration. Someone had asked a question, maybe some General from the Air Force or the Army, she was not sure. As President, she did not think she could let any remark go past her if she did not understand it. She would have to remember to ask the General what that was all about; asking was always awkward, seems she was always being told she had been briefed about whatever it was at some prior meeting…

Strykopolos himself was, at that very moment, fulminating into the small clip-on mic in the secure room of his consulting firm just off the Hill that he opened upon his retirement. He had taken an unobtrusive old building on the far side of the Capitol, as a matter of instinct. He did not need to impress anyone with the address, and the fewer Beltway types he ran into the better. He did not need to network for more clients. With the client he already had, his business had all it would ever need. Besides, under the guise of a gut rehab he could harden the building electronically and physically without attracting attention. City Inspection was not likely to closely compare the architect's stamped plans with the actual work being performed on the structure. Less known, the better.

Strykopolos' take on briefing the President was cynical. As he explained to Carstons, "yeah, well, you see there are always two sides to every argument and our President always opts for the third one, which is to send us back for more analysis. Just so long as she can say she met with the Chiefs and that it was informative, that's all she needs. On that subject, the press doesn't really expect to get anywhere. It's national fucking security after all, so whaddaya expect, the President to lay out our strategy to *USA Today*? They just roll over and start asking her about immigration again."

The General lit up a cigarette and let it hang between his fingers. He was old school, but his mistress had nagged him until he actually paid attention enough to notice that when he was tense he leaned towards chain smoking his filter-less European cancer sticks. Carstons' voice at the other end of the line was measured, calm.

"We may need to execute, at least at some level. Those morons can't protect their balls from their own dicks. They lost another city today, you know, the one that begins with P and sounds like a soft fart? The cities don't much matter until you look at the theater maps and then, Jesus H. Christ, it's all about them with just a few little cross-hatched areas we control. And you should see where those areas are—far from the water, far from Israel. Our strategic positioning is untenable. We need to establish some new kind of boundaries, or they will eat our lunch every day for the rest of our lives."

The General paused. Might as well let the Senators know. "We are pretty well set if that's our direction." He decided to use his military jargon; it always made him feel superior to these lousy political types. "I mean, we have interpersonal redundancy and high technological capability with controls for backsplash. Our people are all trained and are in primary and secondary positions so no one can really interfere with the operation if we choose to go that way."

"I'm worried about getting back-doored by a leak or by some sloppy execution." Carstons' voice was almost hushed, confidential, deeply concerned.

"There won't be any execution issues I tell you. I mean, you and I, we know nothing is 100% ever, but from a, well, military standpoint it ain't gonna get no better." The ash hit the desktop and turned to whitish powder against the glossy polished wood.

Might as well tell him all of it, Strykolopos thought. "Uh, yesterday we addressed the issue of informational security also. I think we are pretty good on that front."

A pause. "What do you mean, exactly?"

Not on this line even though it is the best line, the General thought as he brushed the ashes onto the oriental carpet, taking care to avoid his suit pants. All he said was, "I mean we are pretty good on that front." He breathed out and added, "right up to the highest level of informational risk."

"Well, I hope you are correct, General. After all, it is not only your life and my life we are talking about. There are a lot of people lined up here."

Strykopolos snorted and ground down on the remaining stub of tobacco with his left thumb, oblivious to the hot burning tip he was macerating into the wide crystal ashtray. Sure, the guy on the line would have some explaining to do but he had protection going upward. And the people upward, they were upwind and into the zone of deniability. All everyone had to do was point down towards Gregory Strykopolos and take a skate. Everyone below Gregory Strykopolos, the President's personal advisor, was only taking orders passed down through ranking military officers, and those ranking officers would believe that they were being directed by the President of the United States, according to the protocols Gergory Strykopolos alone had arranged and managed.

Everyone gets an alibi except me, the General thought. How did that work out that way, if I am so goddamned smart, he groused to himself, leaving my own ass hanging out?

"I know, Carstons, I know," the General said. "Everyone has an important stake here. I am on top of it, just don't worry about it. Leave the, uh, the details to me." Deep breath. "Just remember that when it goes down, who made it go down."

The voice replied in the same measured tone, a tone that made the General wince as he clicked the toggle that controlled his mic: "Oh, we won't forget no matter how this turns out. No fear of that."

The General sat in his secure room for a while, absorbing the absolute serenity of total quiet. He lit another cigarette and purposefully smoked it, drawing the dry warmth into his lungs in hungry regular drafts. He needed an old-time feeling of comfort. He also had some detective work to do, and how to get that done was a matter of some uncertainty. Although it was convenient that Caleb McCabe had met his end, as it had been a subject of some discussion for a while, and although it was convenient for the General to report the death as a matter-of-fact accomplishment in furtherance of the enterprise, the General decided that he really would love to know who the hell had actually killed the guy.

At the same time that Strykopolos was walking through his outer office towards his car, Lyle Vincent placed his arm gently around the shoulder of the grieving widow of his dear friend Caleb. It was happenstance that their friend from Massachusetts was visiting them when Caleb was prematurely and cruelly taken. Susannah and the boys needed all the comfort they could get, and a face from home, particularly one who, over time, had become such a good and caring neighbor before the McCabes made the move to Virginia, was truly reassuring.

Susannah tried to blow her nose into a small soggy tissue so she could answer the phone ringing in the den. She glanced down and gulped back a tear as the screen announced that Lois Harding was calling her from Newton. She did not wonder how Lois had gotten the news so quickly; it never occurred to her.

But Lyle Vincent did wonder. He wondered a lot. Just when he thought he knew where all the players fit, someone he did not know had moved his game avatar out of turn.

18

Johnston stepped off the airplane in one big hurry. He had arranged for a watch on the McCabe home once Caleb was found dead, and the CIA photographs sent to his office contained one surprise face among entering mourners: Lyle Vincent. Johnston had never been able to figure out Vincent's history, although he did show up as an electronics salesman for a small firm about which little information was available, but nothing out of the ordinary. Thereafter a divorce proceeding against him was noted, and he continued to live in Newton, alone in his house, and clearly befriended the McCabe family which made Johnston all the more curious and, indeed, outright suspicious.

But Johnston could find nothing further, a few inquiries indicated Vincent had indeed sold circuit boards to a couple of companies in New Jersey and deposits to his bank account seemed by timing and amount to look like appropriate sales commissions. When the McCabes moved to Virginia and, after three months, Vincent had remained in residence at Windwood Circle, and had befriended the family that moved into the former McCabe house, Johnston had discontinued the watch on Vincent. After four years, he could not convince himself that Vincent, curious as he might be, was nefarious.

Until now. Too much of a coincidence, Caleb buying it, with Vincent in town and swooping in so quickly.

Over the years, the Agency had been able to gather some information through the FBI about the McCabe lab before the lab was abruptly decommissioned. Money from the defense budget, in large amounts, seemed to have been applied out of a black ops account, to support a robust scientific inquiry. The problem with that path was that it led to several dead ends. The people working in the lab seemed unremarkable. The suit-wearing liaison was finally identified as Peter Carstons, ex-Army, a mid-level career science officer with DOD. DOD explained that the lab effort was aborted when the McCabe team, after many years, had failed to find anything dangerous in various strains of virus which had been intercepted from a couple of covert labs in Syria. McCabe was supposed to be some expert in all things viral, and had reported that he had ended up exhaustively studying a long list of wholly innocuous viral strains. McCabe had returned to Harvard, and then was retained as a consultant by DOD and had moved to the Washington area when his youngest son was accepted at UVA.

It looked like a couple of dead ends, until now. Johnston had lost a good man in Massachusetts a few years back, and it ate at him. Something was, had been wrong, but he could never discover the whole story. It was a shame Simpson had never been able to fill in any of the blanks. Johnston was sure Simpson had at least some sense of the game that might have been in play, but that seemed to have died with him.

Now McCabe also was dead, and the local police had a store security camera that seemed to show a pick-up truck sliding across a couple of lanes at speed and wiping him out quite convincingly, then fleeing the scene.

An hour after landing at Reagan, Johnston was ringing the doorbell of Susannah McCabe's house in Alexandria. He had a .38 caliber handgun in his right jacket pocket; his Agency backup was around the rear of the house. Many cars were parked outside. Lyle Vincent's Lexus with Massachusetts plates was nowhere in sight.

A woman he did not recognize opened the door. He said he was a friend of the deceased and was admitted to a crowded foyer letting out into a living room on the left, a small dining room on the right with its table covered with cold cuts and salads. Several people were pulled up around the table eating from paper plates, their dishes interspersed with the various food platters. On a credenza, a plastic tablecloth was topped with sodas, a bottle of rye whiskey, a bowl with some ice cubes floating over the melted water, a pair of silver tongs floating inside the bowl with the finger-holds sunk inconveniently down to the bottom of the icy mass.

Johnston poured himself a Fanta, passed on the ice, and slowly moved to the archway of the dining room to glimpse into the living room. No familiar faces. He slid, with an apology, to the swinging doorway opening to the kitchen and gently nudged it open. The kitchen was full of people, some holding drinks or paper plates, most just talking quietly in small clumps. He saw Susannah and the boys over by the sink, which was piled with glasses, used paper plates, and a pile of white plastic dinnerware in a small heap on the drainboard. No sign of Vincent. He retraced his way to the front door, slowly walked to the driveway and street, nursing his soda, looking at the cars. He walked down the driveway and located his backup in the corner of the yard trying to look casual, holding a soda can. In response to Johnston's gesture, he shook his head in the negative.

As he walked to the front, the older McCabe boy came out and ambled down to the street; getting some air, Johnston surmised. Johnston approached him quietly. "You must be Gordy," he said softly. He stuck out his hand. "Your dad was very proud of you, proud of both you boys. Sorry for your loss."

Gordy limply shook the hand, dropping it after two weak pumps. He turned as if to go.

"Say, I thought Lyle Vincent was going to be here. Have you seen him? He called me about this—thing that happened."

"Yeah," Gordy replied with some distraction. "Mr. Vincent was here earlier in the day, he was staying at the house actually. Haven't seen him in the last hour or two. I can ask mom…"

"Oh, no need, you have enough going on. I'll go back in and look around."

Johnston worked his way back in, asked a couple of people if there was another bathroom upstairs until someone replied affirmatively, and walked slowly up to the second floor. As he hit the top of the landing, he put his hand on his pistol and walked down the hall silently, his shoes cushioned by the deep pile of wall-to-wall carpeting. He gently pushed open doors, a bathroom empty, a master bedroom empty, another bathroom empty, an empty boy's room, an empty small office, the last door opened to what was clearly a guest room, the bed lightly made with a throw loosely covering the mattress and pillow. There was no one there. Quietly Johnston opened first the closet, then the dresser drawers. There was no luggage and no clothing. There was no sign of Lyle Vincent. Or whatever his real name was. It would be good to check the room for prints. On his cell phone he called for a forensic aide, who was to present himself as a work colleague of the deceased and find his way up to the end of the second-floor hallway.

Johnston was about to sit on the bed and decided that was not a smart step. He was sorry he had touched so many things already, but his prints could be sorted out. He would wait in the room to keep it secure. If anyone else came in, he would need to think of a story, a headache, a need for a nap perhaps.

Johnston stood in the middle of the room for almost two hours before the forensics agent pushed open the guest room door.

19

Senator Lionel King Darwimple III had, by choice, one of the smallest offices in the Senate Office Building. He chose to meet constituents, those few who managed to get to D.C. from Alabama, in suitably humble quarters. The Senator felt his people would be more comfortable in such quarters and, further, it was a reminder to himself that he may have come pretty far, but not all the way to the top.

His desk was old oak from his law office, shipped North at his insistence and expense. There were the gouges from his son's pocketknife, a couple of splinters from when his law clerk had dropped a brass bookend by accident, and in the front, the bullet hole in the modesty panel from the night when he had been elected to Congress to the displeasure of many, including the still-anonymous shooter. Now at the end of his second and last term, the Senator had been a minor voice, mouthpiece and sometimes trophy exhibit for the Republican Party, although his politics had little to do with their platform and lots to do with his steadfast belief that programs and preferences for Black people were fundamentally inconsistent with future equality of all peoples. His late wife often told him he was a fool to use his personal history to generalize a social theory of economics and politics, but (he often thought) if you could not extrapolate from what you knew, what other basis did you have for an opinion on anything?

As a minority member of the Special Oversight Committee on Science, an appointment particularly ill-suited to his skill set and designed, he suspected, to keep him hidden from substantive matters where he might prove unpredictable, the Senator had struggled to understand the new technologies that seemed to lay claim to governmental dollars. The nanotech stuff he could intuit if not understand; the biotech was another matter. He had reluctantly taken a white aide, against his instinct, because James J. McCarthy had majored in biochemistry at Yale. Each made the other uncomfortable in ways they could not exactly define. While not condescending, McCarthy sometimes showed curt impatience as the Senator rubbed his bald-shaven head, pulled his vest down over his unfortunately sagging stomach, and asked again about how the spliced genes affected the health of people already of adult age. As for the Senator, he just did not like anyone who went to Yale.

But tonight the Senator was more than usually perplexed, so much so that he chose not even to share his questions with his aide. At the last hearing on virus containment, a senior Senator not known for his command of cutting-edge science, had asked how the containment research on that new biologic enhancer that came out of Boston was coming. He had a distinct impression that a couple of senior staff members jumped when the question came out, and one hastened to note that that subject would be handled "off-line at a later date."

Darwimple had a practice of not speaking at informal

meetings and closed hearings, lest he disclose lack of knowledge. But, trained to be a lawyer and thus not comfortable with being in the neighborhood of something he did not understand, he had asked his aide to gather a file on matters relating to that inquiry. He held the file in his hand. The science was cryptic, full of jargon, but some parts of the file were most interesting. Interesting indeed. Aside from the money which had been spent on this project, which was substantial, was the source: the Department of Defense. What was the military doing with biologic research?

He made a note to ask McCarthy to locate this Dr. McCabe, who had headed the project, and who fortuitously seems to have relocated to the Washington area. Rising to go home, the Senator glanced down at the file. Unlike most of what he saw, particularly as it affected the military, it was not just marked as Classified. Some of the papers inside also were marked "Top Secret." He also told himself to remember to ask McCarthy how he had gotten that group of papers copied. There was an undercurrent of lack of security relative to the sciences which also could be the subject of appropriate Congressional investigation, but the Senator quickly relegated that task, in his head, to younger and more energetic Senators who no doubt soon would follow him.

He opened his small safe and slipped the thin file onto the top shelf, underneath the draft budget, on top of a Committee report on cyber security problems with the FDA branch when they handled genetically modified food grains.

"He's dead? When did that happen, I just saw that he was living in D.C.."

"He actually was killed in a bicycle accident yesterday, Senator." McCarthy cleared his throat. "Near his home in Alexandria." As the Senator's aide, McCarthy had learned to "correct" his Senator obliquely. His Senator was very sensitive to being corrected by white young Yale graduates.

"Well, isn't that the damnedest thing?" The Senator rocked back in his chair. "How inconvenient," he muttered to himself. Then, "Please find out who else worked on this, wait a minute, let me find the page… this laboratory—here it is, wait, the page is classified, let me write it down for you."

McCarthy groaned inside, he was no detective, and he could not just call up the FBI or the DOD and get cooperation. The mention of the Darwimple name did not exactly make anyone in government jump to attention and offer assistance. And additionally, he could seldom read the Senator's handwritten jottings.

"Oh, wait a minute, let me print this out for you," said the Senator, "you never seem to be able to know what the hell I write down in plain English for you…"

McCarthy had a social relationship, started online, with one Lilah Greenberg, a young lawyer assigned to the CIA office in D.C. He had trolled J-Date, the Jewish date-matching site, with the clever name "Liberal Goyish Maven," a half-Yiddish phrase given him by a Jewish colleague who had extolled the quality of women on that site. When McCarthy noted that he was obviously not Jewish, he had been advised to use that name and he would attract curious replies from many who would not necessarily find his religious views an impediment.

McCarthy was a lazy sort; there were no doubt normal channels to mount an inquiry, the Senator was after all, in fact, a United States Senator, but reaching out seemed so easy, and he was wanting to get together with Greenberg again, she had been a lot of fun and was perhaps a willing player. He picked up the phone and dialed.

Johnston sat upright in his seat at the briefing report. Why was a United States Senator's office asking about newly deceased Dr. McCabe? Nothing made any sense so what can you do but keep asking questions; you never know. And who was this Greenberg? He found Greenberg in the staff directory and took the elevator down to fifteen to find her office.

20

Johnston had used an intermediary on the Hill to set up his meeting with the Senator. It was agreed that the Senator's calendar would enter Johnston under a false name, so he wouldn't be on any formal visitor's record and the visit could be explained as a meeting with a constituent or as an old acquaintance of the Senator's son who needed a personal favor.

Johnston asked the Senator straight out what his interest might be in one dead biochemist, and the Senator told him that while the Agency might well know damned near everything about almost everything, a Senator is entitled to have an interest in something and keep that interest confidential.

"I might rather ask," continued Darwimple, who for once was sorry his office was so modest, "why the Agency has gone through all this rigmarole just because I asked about this man. In fact, what is your interest in this man?" The Senator allowed a faint smile.

"You know, agent—uh Johnston, some people still think that the United States Senate is more powerful and more important than even your Agency." His eyebrows raised as his Senatorial head lowered, his chin resting on the knot of his tie in pleasure at having made his point so smoothly.

"I will tell you," said Johnston, adopting a tone of intimacy in hopes of defusing the tension. "I am not here to fence or be mysterious. We work for the same boss, you know."

"We have been interested in McCabe for many years. We had heard odd rumors about his laboratory in Massachusetts and could not figure out where the funding came from. We thought it might well be Federal, but then again no one was claiming the baby and I don't like those kinds of loose ends with people messing around with viruses and all."

Be damned, the Senator said to himself. Ain't nobody knows where these guys get their juice, is there? Out loud, he just permitted a "please continue."

"When we realized how much money likely seemed to be involved, I sent an experienced agent to do some field work and one day they found him face down in some friggin' suburban fishpond with what looked like a very professional blow to the back of his head." Johnston paused to see if he could get the Senator to offer anything at this point, but the Senator just gestured with a horizontal hand wave that said "keep going, you have my attention."

"Yes. Well, there is someone else involved in the case, I mean seems someone else also was trying to find out about the lab. Not one of ours. Then nothing happened. I mean, we didn't get any more information, couldn't link anyone to my dead agent, and McCabe started spending more time back lecturing at Harvard. Then the lab closed, and this person we were interested in, he just turned out to be McCabe's next-door neighbor. A bit of a creep but he seemed to check out. Until lately."

The Senator shifted and sat more upright. "Yes, so what happened?"

I wonder if you already know, Johnston thought to himself. "Okay," Johnston continued, "so McCabe shows up dead, a relatively young man, and it comes over the wire because his name trips into my old case list, and the police department here has some film that suggests it wasn't accidental that he was a hit-and-run victim, and I ask for some local back-up and they send me pictures of the sad mourners at the guy's house and there is this original neighbor we couldn't figure out, he happens to be visiting from Massachusetts and staying at the McCabe house when McCabe buys it. And he is pretty cozy with the family, staying there and all."

"So, Senator, here is the thing and why I need to close the loop you have opened. I go to the house, the McCabe house, to check up on my mystery friend, and he's gone."

"Gone? What do you mean, gone?"

"He's just plain gone, doesn't tell anyone, he just disappears. We go to his room and all his personal effects are gone. His toothbrush and comb are gone from the bathroom counter. And now I'm sure he's implicated; although I still don't know with what."

"Tell me, Agent, because this sort of sounds like a grade B, make that a grade C novel on the rack at an airport newsstand, tell me why all of a sudden you are so sure that this guy, who you couldn't implicate in something for years, all of a sudden is so interesting to you?"

"Well, Senator, here's the thing. We dusted for

fingerprints and you know what we found?" The Senator shrugged.

"The only prints in the room were a couple of my own, that I left when I first entered. The man had spent a couple of nights in that room. No way he never touched anything. No way there weren't other people's prints there from beforehand. Senator, the guy wiped down the room. He had reason to suspect he would be identified, and he skipped out and covered his tracks. He's a professional, Senator, and he is not ours."

Johnston paused for a moment, straightened up in his chair, crossed one leg over the other and tried to fix the Senator with his most earnest patriotic gaze.

"So, Senator Darwimple, your country would like to know why all of a sudden you had your staff query the Agency, out of the blue, about my dead man?"

"Shit," said the Senator, as he stood, walked to his wall safe and withdrew his thin file on Caleb McCabe and his laboratory in Cambridge, Massachusetts. He was somehow sure that Johnston would not make an issue out of looking at some pages marked "Top Secret" which even a Senator should not have in his office.

21

President Sarah Louise Peters certainly was smart as hell but seemed extraordinarily ordinary in so many other ways. A Protestant from a tiny New York City suburb, only child of a door-to-door salesman (one of the last of the old-time broom vendors who carried around a selection of "Fuller Brushes" from household to household in an age of burgeoning electronic commerce) and a part-time librarian (the Town Hall was only open three days a week, and the library was in the East Wing). Sarah was near the top of her high school class, had a normal number of normal friends, sang in Glee Club, after three years decided she did not want to sing in Church Choir, won a partial scholarship to Barnard College based on some surprisingly robust College Board test scores which suggested that she might find herself to be pretty successful. Sarah was an art history major and did not particularly apply herself, graduating in the midst of her class, ending up with a boyfriend one year behind her at Columbia and a low-paying job dealing with old English prints at a small gallery on Madison in the upper Sixties.

Sarah was petite, relatively flat in body and aspect, with curly brown hair that she would never let grow out, and a straightforward approach to life that announced that this was a reasonably bright, reasonably nice, reasonably unstylish young woman whom you could trust.

That was then. Unable to have children for reasons unknown and in need of more of something, Sarah became active in the Manhattan Democratic Party, became an unremarkable delegate to two Party conventions where she was lucky enough to be a strong supporter of two ultimately winning candidates for President. With the untimely death of her boyfriend, with whom she had lived for fifteen years but never married—you got married for the children, she would say—Sarah found herself both in need of a higher-paying job and connected to some pretty important Democrats.

Working in D.C. as an aide to Senator Maximilian Looper (Lord Looper to his Republican enemies, Loopy to his Democratic friends, who were many), Sarah rose silently in politics through a late marriage to Loopy, a position on the D.C. City Council, and then as a surprise member of the House of Representatives shortly after her move to Maryland, elected from a newly Democratic district that had been invaded by the people who were making the Democratic Party unbeatable in elections outside the Red States and gerrymandered pockets elsewhere.

Years ago the party was riven by a great schism. Hispanic immigration, Black Lives suddenly mattering, growing pressure from the environmental lobby as the seas once again inundated perpetually unprotectable New Orleans, confusion left by her predecessor, and two years of death and economic chaos from an unthinkable pandemic, all had to be mediated against the people with the money and their hands on the traditional political levers and PACs. There was a great need for someone about whom no one had anything bad to say. Someone decent. Someone who, in the terribly strident milieu of what had become of politics, could stand up and say that criticisms of her were, well, just plain wrong and further, unkind.

Sarah did not try to stay out of trouble during the campaign but she was a candidate who trouble itself seemed to avoid. Everyone including Sarah read the newspapers that morning, swallowed hard at her 49.2% of the popular vote and her narrow Electoral College victory, and here Sarah now sat, having applied in her Presidency her common sense and assiduously solicited political advice to a variety of problems, having done no better but no worse than her more illustrious predecessors. The Republic still had a deficit, modest economic growth, more wind turbines and too many prisoners. Illegal immigrants were still illegal and still in place. Welcome to America.

So it took a lot to rile the President, who had grown a quiet confidence in her own confidence during the past two years or more. But she did not like, as her husband would sometimes remark, to have someone piss on her leg and tell her it was raining. She particularly did not like it when her military aide, General Strykopolos, was clearly covering up something, as was apparent at the Joint Chiefs briefing the day before, a subject she pursued with purpose in the Oval Office the following day.

"So, let me see if I understand this, Gregory," she almost cooed as the General shifted uncomfortably. "When the Colonel from the Air Force…" She paused and looked up.

"That would be Army General Burbridge, I think," the

General offered helpfully.

"Yes, Burbridge. Officious man, but then again there are worse failings I suppose. When Burbridge mentioned that the new delivery system for the new weapons class had to be considered, and you told him it was not germane to the conversation we were having—our conversation was about weapons and how they are delivered, yes?" she asked in what was not a question, and she continued without awaiting an answer, "you now are telling me that you share with me an ignorance of what he was referring to?"

"Madame President, whatever it was, it was not on the briefing sheet so it could not have been important. I figured I would track it down later. We had all the missile deployment issues to deal with, Middle East, Far East, Eastern Europe."

"But General, you are a senior advisor to the Administration. You are a consultant but my people have told me that I should include you as my, well, guru, my 'go-to' expert on what I do not know. And there are so many things that are still alien to me."

Sarah put on the scowl that the General knew was never good news, the scowl that narrowed her eyes and brought out those two indentations above her nose and highlighted the unevenness of her complexion, sallow against her tight brown hair with those growing gray streaks.

"Gregory, that is just unacceptable and, forgive me, I find that I cannot credit it. I actually feel that you are holding back information from me. No doubt you think it is for my own good but, I assure you, it cannot be. So, I am again asking you what that reference was all about." She paused and hissed, "and if I do not get satisfaction, I will have to

find someone else who will tell this commander-in-chief just
what the deuce is going on in her military establishment."

22

Senator Darwimple, a staunch Republican, never much liked the President but, then again, what did that matter? After a couple of years of any presidency no one, whether mere citizen or exalted Senator, ever expressed full confidence in any sitting President. He was indeed surprised, however, to be summoned to the Oval Office for a meeting where, as he was told, "the President has blocked out an hour on a matter of national security." And so soon after his visit from someone from the Agency. Just what in all get-out was going on here, anyway?

"Senator, we've not had much time together, have we?"

"No, Madame President. To my great regret." Darwimple figured, no one disliked a gallant sentiment.

Fuck, he thought, you avoided me like the minor annoyance I am.

"Well, I have this most interesting report from the Central Intelligence Agency involving the late Dr. McCabe. Seems this is one of the cases where the left hand is unaware of the right hand. Or at least the President is unaware of several busy hands."

"Really? Well, that is unfortunate. You know, Madame, we Senators when we do not understand what is going on, we just assume the Executive branch is up to its tricks again." Dear me, thought Darwimple, clearly phrased too strongly, she IS the President.

"That is to say," he hastened, "figuratively speaking."

"Yes. Well, I think I understand. I was in the House myself, you may recall."

Off the hook, the Senator allowed with relief an "ah—yes."

"And, Madame President, if I may be so bold, how is it that the CIA is involved in an inquiry which seems wholly domestic? The Senate has of late become sensitive to the seeming creep of the CIA into matters internal to the United States, as its mandate is not on American soil."

Sarah leaned forward, decided to ignore the question, and lowered her voice. "Senator, I am very concerned about something which came up at a recent—well, let us call it a meeting. It seems that, notwithstanding treaty obligations and the stated policy of our country under many Presidents, there was some sort of a germ warfare operation going on, and it was known to the military, and perhaps to the State Department, and no doubt to others whom I do not now know, but not to the Executive Office. And, incredibly, I am being stonewalled. By my own advisors. Most unsettling…"

"Ah—yes?"

"Yes indeed. And it turns out that the CIA and the FBI have been similarly confounded, actually for several years, but that very lack of information has kept the issue off the briefings I receive. If someone hadn't really misspoken the other day, I would still be totally in the dark."

"Ah, yes?"

"Yes indeed. But seemingly you were not in the dark, were you, Senator? When our agent, uh" glancing down at a single sheet of typing on her desk pad, "Agent Johnston met with you the other day, you seemed to have a file all about this, shall we say, operation?"

"Madame, we may be of different parties, and I may be a minor player in Washington, but I must assure you that I am not party to anything untoward." The Senator paused, waited for and received a nod of acquiescence and understanding from his President.

"I myself just recently stumbled over this—anomaly. My committee is science oversight, you know. I asked my assistant to dig up some information, and he came up with some sketchy information and I wanted more. Instead of using channels, if you will, he made a personal call to a friend at the CIA and one thing led to another and, well, here we are. All I know I told that Johnston. There was this laboratory for years, it was funded to the level of nine figures at least, the money came out of the black box part of the military budget, and McCabe was an academic into viruses. I do not know, as I sit here, what he did or did not develop, who commissioned the work, or whether indeed it is virus warfare or germ warfare or something to protect our troops in the field from, hell, diarrhea."

Sarah smiled and leaned back in her chair. "Senator, whatever it is, I assure you it is nothing so benign as that. People readily tell me about all sorts of, well, bullshit, pardon the language. They only hide things from me when they are very sensitive. And important."

"Madame President, I assume you have access now to

the information I had in my file. What can I do to assist you? This does not strike me as a partisan moment."

"No indeed, Senator. Military operations unknown to the commander-in-chief with multi-year existence and hundreds of millions of dollars of budget are not political in the common sense. They are serious and structural, if you will. So here is what I want you to do. I will alert Democratic members of your Committee that they are to support you as you call an immediate hearing on the subject of this McCabe laboratory. I will designate an aide to liaise with you and assist you in any way necessary. I want a wide number of people under oath to testify, including the military. The Department of Justice will be at your disposal in the face of any resistance, either constitutionally or otherwise. I intend to make secrecy here untenable. Untenable, Senator. And I need your help."

"Madame, political suicide, which is what you are placing on my shoulders, is a welcome burden to this retiring Senator who just wants to go home. Of course I will do it. I will do it at once, President Peters."

"I didn't think you wouldn't, frankly. Your—reputation is of candor and honesty, Senator." The President paused for a moment, and added with a thin smile, "for a Republican, that is…"

23

Army General Spears had no idea what was being asked of him. He knew of course that he was to arrange to take a tanker up the North River in Boston and tie it up to what was described as a crude oil tank that did not contain any crude oil. And await further instructions. He was to be in charge of this effort, although the ship was naval and was to be manned by naval personnel. He was to select an elite force of combat-ready Green Berets to guard the ship while in transit and while docked. He was to keep all of this at the highest level of security, although that last instruction seemed a bit over-the-top, as in fact he did not think he knew anything of a sensitive nature. What the hell was going on, anyway?

General Spears turned to his aide, Colonel Detwiler, and said in a low, confidential voice, "we have some orders to go active, but stateside. This is top secret, comes from the Joint Chiefs. Don't ask me questions, I only know what I am telling you. I need, if you can believe it, fully equipped teams of Berets to provide 24-7 security for a vessel of a length of 750 feet, both at sea and while docked. Whaddaya think? How many troops do I need?"

Detwiler was career, as was General Spears. Spears wore only one star after all these years, likely a reflection of his outspoken nature, but a good soldier, all professional and spit and polish. Old school. Detwiler liked old school. But this was, well, odd.

"A vessel sir? You mean, like a ship? A naval ship?" Detwiler's brow scrunched in confusion.

"Yes, that's right."

"Berets, not Seals?"

"That's what I am ordered. Seems to be some inter-branch operation."

"And where are we going? If it's the Middle East we may need air and…"

"Boston," Spears interrupted. He looked down at his desk, the conversation was so bizarre as to embarrass him even before his friend and subordinate.

"Boston like in Massachusetts?" Incredulity dripped from the question.

"Yes, Colonel, Boston. Of course, Massachusetts. We pick up the vessel in Groton, Connecticut, to which it is now en route, exactly six days from now, together with our complement of troops. We will be housed on the vessel, which can accommodate any number of men we designate. We sail directly to Boston, a trip that will take about 20 hours. We tie up alongside our destination and await orders. That's it."

"Well, I'll be damned. Are we expecting any actual threat? Is there a formal alert? Is this a terrorist thing? How do you suggest we equip our force? Do we need air cover?"

"How the hell do I know?" The General was annoyed, mainly because he knew so little. Lack of knowledge destroyed preparation, and preparation was the essential element of success. What was he defending against?

"I think we should assume maximum alert. I mean, I don't envision a large number of people we should be prepared to deal with, but I think this is a silent op so we aren't thinking just protesters here. Let's assume a well-armed small adverse strike force. We need night capability, small and medium arms, and surveillance at all times. Short duty, don't want anyone losing focus. Robust communications; since we don't know anything, we gotta be prepared to deal with everything conceivable." The General paused.

"Never thought of air support, however. I'll ask up the chain and advise. So what do you think?"

Detwiler stood up a bit straighter. He always liked to be in the military moment when he was acting military. "Well, sir, I figure four-hour rotation, pairs every fifty feet, fourteen teams so that's twenty-eight people times six. That's what, about 160-something, plus officers." He paused, forgetting his military bearing.

"Sir, doesn't that strike you as a hell of a lot of people to watch a boat tied up in Boston Harbor?"

"Colonel, nothing strikes me as anything except to do Job One. Figure out your staffing and report back by oh-nine-hundred tomorrow with specifics. And as you do this, no information is to be given out, you understand?"

"Yessir."

"And Colonel, get used to calling it a ship, will you? Those Navy guys are pretty sensitive about it."

He got his "yessir" back and, as Detwiler started to wheel, the General reached out and stopped him with a hand on his shoulder.

"Colonel, I don't know what this is about, but it seems to be pretty important. I was told we will be provided with information about the Corps of Engineers who will be working on the ship, and we are not to interfere. I have no idea what engineers have to do with this, so don't bother to ask. They also are digging a deeper channel in the harbor for our ship, Lou. Can you believe that?" Spears dropped his voice and said, half to himself, "this may be really serious shit going down…"

"Yessir," said Detwiler. Then, "a pleasure to be in your command again, General."

Spears nodded. Maybe not, he thought. But he just returned the salute and watched Detwiler step smartly through the doorway, closing it with a firm click behind him.

Spears thought, I should contact my brother in Boston, a good chance to have dinner, catch up with each other's family. Then immediately he decided that that wasn't very consistent with maximum security.

24

Orders were orders. Spears had been reminded of that several times in his career, and in a manner that suggested that he should know better than to ask so many questions. But he did graduate the Academy at the top of his class, loved the arias from Puccini, haunted the National Gallery, viewed himself as a Renaissance warrior to the extent such a person existed. He sometimes admitted to himself, after his wife was upstairs in bed and he was in his small den with his Knob Hill, neat, a gentleman's bourbon, that he was not only different from but better than his fellow officers. The number of stars did not make the man, but rather the man's mind was the true measure.

And his mind was troubled. First, the basic order was bizarre on its face. Next, it did not come from Naval Central Command (USCENTCOM), or from USNORTHCOM, but from USSOUTHCOM; Vice Admiral Lefrak, the Deputy Commander. Spears was to staff the Berets from whatever resources he thought best. He had tapped Detwiler for that, good man, based out of the Military District of Washington at Fort McNair, no problem there.

And the orders relative to the vessel originated with USPACOM, the Pacific Command. And yet the ship was out of Norfolk, the mobile logistics support force for the Atlantic. How did the Pacific command get the authority to assign out of the Atlantic fleet? It made no sense and, further, suggested a level of coordination that was generally not exhibited by the still-segmented command structure notwithstanding efforts to coordinate.

Next morning, unable to settle his mind, Spears reached out to the office of the Defense Secretary for some clarification. It was outside command structure, almost like an overt questioning of his orders, but at this point he figured he had his one and only star and so it was not like his career was at risk. He knew Patterson, or was it Peterson, at the Office of Intelligence Oversight; might as well start there. He located Peterson, Laurence in his computer; they had shared some time at War College a long time ago. Then he thought, how do I phrase my inquiry so it does not escalate beyond setting my own mind at ease?

Spears wrote: "Dear Larry, Long time no talk; hope all is well. We should find time for lunch now that both of us are here in D.C.. But I am writing for a clarification. Got orders to support a vessel out of Norfolk with a Green Beret cohort. Orders were cut out of Southern Pacific Command, not USCENTCOM which I would have expected. And troop protection, though it is bound for Boston. Is there a security overlay here? No one gave me detail but not sure I can properly staff without more and thought you might have an insight. Let me know, if you will. Thanks."

Spears knew Peterson would read between the lines; that Spears wanted information and did not want to piss off the officers up the line by questioning orders. But

DOD administration was not the uniformed military, they understood and often mediated these kinds of inquiries and issues.

So it was of some surprise when, within the hour, he received an encrypted email from the Under Secretary for Acquisition, Technology and Logistics: "Re inquiry to Intelligence Oversight, referred here 0930 today, be advised orders confirmed per Central Command. Direct any further inquiry Admiral Lionel Catchings, Vice Chair Joint Chiefs. Technical data needed should be requested 455th Chemical Brigade, U.S. Army Reserve, Dix, copy Catchings."

Be damned, thought Spears. When did secretive and hidebound Intelligence bounce an inquiry to another office, and so quickly? And what the hell was the reference to the 455th? Should I go to Lefrak at Southern Command, forget subtlety and demand the information? Not a comfortable thought, nothing to do with promotions or no promotions. Just not, well, old school. Spears would have to cogitate a bit and decide if he would just follow the orders, or find another path to uncover what was happening and, now with reference to the 455th, what was going to be inside that vessel. Maybe he should tell Detwiler to get some serious armament to avoid close approach by other vessels. And what about air cover; maybe he needed air after all. But his orders did not mention air. What the hell was going on?

It took a second glass of bourbon for the idea to hit Spears. He had a lot of respect for a Senator whom he had met several times on the Hill, a minor player to be sure but a bright guy with a remarkably candid and open approach to things. And with the 455th involved, Senator Darwimple might have a clue and he was, indeed, not in the chain of command so no worries there. The Senator was on the Science Committee; Spears had appeared a couple of times, once about the lead in bullets, once explaining the use of asbestos in Humvees. Sure, in a direct hit the asbestos particles would fill the air but, with a direct hit, asbestos particles were the least of the problems. He recalled clearly the visible wince Darwimple showed in response to his answer.

25

Darwimple had no idea what General Spears was talking about, and told the General that it was unlikely he would have any insight; would the General like to talk to the Senate Armed Forces Committee? The General said he would NOT like; a quick goodbye ensued. What a curious week this was, thought the Senator, full of disconnected mysteries. First, a summons from the President herself. Now an inquiry from the Army. Why, he had not had so much confusion in all of his two dull terms in the Congress put together. Nor was it his intention to poke around for information; after all, he would not even know where to poke. Ships of the fleet went all over the place all of the time.

Carlos Vincente looked at Detwiler with the same expression Detwiler had given to Spears.

"We are providing security to a ship going to fucking Boston?" He paused and added, "Sir?"

"That is right, Master Sergeant."

"Colonel, we are a Green Beret unit. We are going from Connecticut to Massachusetts and tying up at an oil tank and we are to provide 24-7 high alert security?"

"That is correct, Master Sergeant," Detwiler said with the start of a grin. He knew that Vincente, his choice to designate specific units, was having the very same reaction he had had when talking with General Spears.

"Uh, speak freely?"

"Certainly."

"Why?"

"Well, Master Sergeant, if I knew I am sure I would not be able to tell you, but in fact I do not know. And the General may know because he called me first thing this morning and specified that he wanted to be able to repel approaching ships at some distance so there would be no chance of, well, being rammed."

"Rammed?" Vincente swallowed, sucked in air so he could find his voice. "Rammed? Berets on a vessel, Berets on the shore, are supposed to stop a vessel that is—how many hundreds of feet long—from being rammed? Do we have air support? Anything that floats?"

"Not that I know of." Detwiler stood up from his desk, came around and planted his butt on the corner, pushing a small stack of papers half across the surface.

"Look, it's weird. It's going to stay weird. The only hope we have is that it doesn't get any more weird. Just let's do it like we're in, well, the Army, know what I mean?"

"Yessir. Sure. How many men you think?"

Detwiler sighed. "I originally thought about 200, even though that seems absurdly high. Then with the email this morning from Spears—encrypted no less—I'm thinking 200 with conventional weaponry but also four teams with night-equipped mobile missile ordinance. And maybe some shore patrol and some high-tech sensor capability. I'm beginning to think we should staff as if we were guarding a military vessel in hostile territory. Just in case, mind you."

"Yessir. Another question?"

"Go on."

"We ought to have a senior officer on duty throughout. If this is as weird as I, well, whatever, then we gotta assume we don't know shit but that it's important. Can I suggest, sir, that you designate personnel at the captain rank to serve as senior officers on duty at all times?"

Detwiler smiled. The entire operation reeked of cluster-fuck, why not play it to the hilt.

"I will consider it, Master Sergeant. And, you are dismissed. Report back 1800 with status." He saluted Vincente out the door and, as it closed, picked up the phone and dialed a number from memory.

"Captain Stoneman? This is Detwiler, D.C. District."

Something was said at the other end that made Detwiler laugh out loud.

"Yeah, you too. So, how the hell are you doin', Roberta?"

Something on the other end again.

Then, "well I think that may have to wait. I have a mission and I need some support. From someone with the discipline to take the mission seriously. But, not over the phone. Tonight at 7?"

26

Panos had no idea what was going on within his project. He was not even sure he knew why he was still employed at the Defense Advanced Research Projects Agency; he was well past retirement age—well past indeed—but he kept getting "extended," and told to interface through Carstons. "You're just too essential to retire, Lance," Carstons would say every time Panos raised the subject. Panos always wondered how Carstons came to that conclusion.

That was doubly strange since the Secretary of Defense himself had instructed Panos that Carstons was seconded from DOD and was in full charge of this DARPA project on a "permanent, long-term basis." At that point, and ever since, life had been strange and Carstons his ubiquitous superior.

This rainy morning Panos gently tested his leg muscles before he tried to get out of bed. For most of his life, his routine had been to flip over the cover, swing his body, drop his feet to the floor and charge onward. But around 70 he found that he was getting cramps in his calves. Now, he had to carefully focus on each leg and give it a tentative stretch, heel out, toe up, feeling for a start of a twinge, relieving the pressure for a moment if he felt a cramp coming on.

Satisfied with his legs, Panos sat up slowly in his bed. He told himself his routine was designed to be careful not to wake his wife, but his mind knew better; it was in fact designed to ease himself upwards and avoid that dizzy moment when he needed to reach out and brace himself on his end table so that he did not pitch over onto the floor.

Stabilized at last, Panos slipped into his scuffs; he preferred slippers with backs to them, but putting them on required bending down to pull up the heel, and the less bending the better. I am eighty-six, he thought, and lucky to be alive so, no complaints. Quietly closing the bedroom door, he shuffled down the hall to the kitchen and put the water on to boil. He spooned a double dose of coffee grinds into the French press; today he would spend the morning at home, reviewing recent "developments."

Seated at the table, his back to the sliders, his garden over his shoulder not allowed to call him hither—not today—he opened the folder marked "Defense Advanced Research Projects Agency – Maximum Top Secret – Project V." On top was yesterday's message from Carstons, decrypted by his assistant. He had an "emergency additional allocation" to Project V, which was strange since Panos thought that V was just about completed. But more curious still was the staggering amount: $3.2 billion. How was that possible? DARPA's budget had increased steadily over the years, to be sure, but this amount was inexplicable. It was, what, about half the entire annual funding for the whole Agency, all 52 open projects.

And not only was the "why" beyond comprehension, so was the "how." Sure, Carstons always seemed able to get whatever project funding V needed, even when things were dicey in the early years, never a pushback, never a question. But prior funding, while large, had not seemed out of scale for the Agency—until now.

Panos let his memory carry him back to the early days. The Agency had been through so many changes, from name to mission to levels of funding. When Panos first joined in 1958, inspired by Ike's call to assist the country in confronting the Soviet's space program following the surprise launch of Sputnik, the Agency had welcomed Panos and his impressive doctorate from MIT at the age of 21, and assigned him to the team evaluating new technologies vying for financial support out of the then impressive $250,000,000 budget.

I'm the only one remaining from that first year, Panos thought. Flattering indeed, but why? Why is it all so confusing to know what is happening when I've been part of the Project for over 20 years?

And who the hell was Carstons anyway? He did not show up on the DARPA org chart, nor anywhere else in the DOD listings. He had his own office, which seemed to be a civilian office, in D.C. He had worked with—probably "for"—Carstons for what, about two decades now and he knew as little about the man today as he knew at the beginning. That was when Carstons brought a folder marked "Project V" to his office and showed him a proposal from a Dr. McCabe in Boston. A doctor whom thereafter Panos had funded and supervised for more than twenty years, who had just died he had been told, and whom he had—incredible now to think of it—never even met.

And what really was V about? The DARPA mission since the Cold War began had been funding transformative science for the defense of the Nation. V did not seem to fit. In fact, in the beginning, there was not even a relevant program office for it. Carstons had explained that because V did not neatly fit, the Agency Director had designated a special status for V and had named Panos as Special Deputy Director, an office that also did not appear on the DARPA org chart. And just recently, Panos happened to glance at that org chart, and could not find his name at all, not in the Adaptive Execution Office where he had been seemingly assigned according to the Agency directory, not anywhere.

Panos fingered the file. When he finally decided to review it, he realized it was a serious breach of Agency Directives to take the file from the building. All of his other files were in their locked drawers in his office, and Panos placed a dummy file he had made up for Project V, containing some innocuous old pages, just in case someone opened his file cabinet—of course, everyone knew that security had the keys and combinations for everything.

God, Panos thought, I have been at this far far too long; look at me, I am totally paranoid here, I actually made up a separate file because—why?—why of course, I am scared because I do not know what to be scared about.

He once had responsibilities, in the past, beyond Project V. During the Cold War era he had worked on missile systems, detection systems, night vision research. Even when V first started, he also was assigned responsibility for early robotics projects, anti-tank devices, software designed to evaluate massive data sets collected from battlefield sensors. But over the last few years, he had been asked—told—to just concentrate on V; if it wasn't a 40-hour a week job that's okay, you're a senior guy, hell you deserve a lightened load, but you are too valuable to leave because of V, so just go with it Lance, and by the way the Special Deputy Directorship comes with a special pay scale that also reflects seniority. Yeah, funny, I agree that the total number is more than the Director but then again he has been here 5-6 years and you Lance what is it, my Lord is it really six decades, is that even possible?…

Panos had tried to get involved in some of the sexy new stuff, which lately he learned about only from the intra-Agency general newsletters. People were working on rockets, jet packs, robots, even now biologics; why not move V to the Biological Technologies Office, he had asked, when that new program was opened in, when was that, 2015? Oh no, he was told, BTO has a full plate and besides you have the history with Project V so let's leave it where it is under your supervision. He had mentioned that the skill sets of the people at BTO were a better fit for V, he was a Ph.D. in chemistry not life sciences, but he kept getting the same answer.

Panos returned to the V file. On top, the notice of new funding. Under that, a message announcing the sad passing of Dr. McCabe, chief scientist for V, and the particularly curious last paragraph: "Henceforth, all communications about this Project are to be directed, encrypted and top secret, to Mr. Carstons, with a copy to General G. Strykopolos (ret.)."

What in the Sam Hill is going on? Carstons knows nothing about the technology, and Panos' communications were related to the substance of the work. And he had looked up the General; an inactive military ex-general, Northeast Command. Inactive military? Advisor to the President?

Only one thought stuck in his mind: they were trying to militarize V. Always a possibility of course given Agency mandate but, "inactive" duty General? More troubling still, why were certain people with no seemingly official portfolio, or existence, intimately involved in the chain of command? Were those nutbags planning to deploy? Whom could he ask? Was it any of his business? Was he going to be asked to take responsibility for releasing the new multi-billion-dollar funding? DARPA was immune by statute from most of the government's bidding and expenditure controls, and V had long ago been removed from the public projects roster (along with some other projects best left undiscussed), but if this was going to implementation, he wanted no part of it. He had the chilling thought that he was being set up, the guy who would look like the man who pushed the button.

I wish to hell I had retired, he thought. This is what my ego has gotten me into. Now, how do I extract myself?

The next day, as Panos sat in his study reading the funding history of Project V, Carstons' assistant handed Carstons a note which caused him to rock back in his chair. "Good God, what else could possibly go wrong," he said softly. And he thought to himself, I was half afraid of this.

He reread the note: "Panos file V out of the building per chip scan." Carstons folded the note, placed it in his breast pocket, and called for his limo.

27

1588 Q Northwest was indistinguishable within the row of gentrified brick three-story town houses that marched primly up and down the block, both sides of the street. Nor, for that matter, from the other brick three stories in the refurbished Northwest, where a plethora of embassies and a few glassy high-rise apartment buildings stuck upward from the original middle-class houses now broken into one-floor apartments. The town houses were occupied by civil servants, lobbyists, entrepreneurs and law professors, who decorated mixing modern Italian light fixtures and sleek bathrooms into the narrow high-ceilinged rooms with the tile-faced fireplaces and ceiling moldings. In compact square front yards, set behind low stone walls, random plantings alongside stone stairs vied for sunlight with a few vestigial perennials and untrimmed bushes.

1588 was maintained to look typical from the outside. About the only thing different was the lot in the rear, occupied solely by an old garage. A short, tarred driveway, the entire width of that lot, led to a nondescript low brick garage with dual, dilapidated gray wooden doors. Anyone who cared to notice might be surprised by the automatic opening of those doors on those rare occasions when cars, generally newer model black vehicles with darkly tinted windows, rolled slowly onto the short driveway. Or further surprised by the apparent depth of the garage which, in fact, ran almost the full dimension of the lot, abutted the rear wall of 1588, and was capable of absorbing four vehicles, two in each row.

Other hidden attributes of 1588 similarly were not apparent. The wooden garage doors were lined with tempered steel. The bulletproof window glass seemed ordinary from the street. The metal rolled shutters were mounted out of sight on the inside of the building. The doors were lined with one inch steel and had bolts that sank 12 inches into metal jambs. There were no electronic leaks out of the building. Aiming a listening device at the building produced a strange, constant low hum. The basement contained a propane generator with enough stored gas to sustain the interior for weeks.

When, upon a neighbor's complaint, a D.C. building inspector rang the bell at 1588 to inquire about the apparent lack of rear line set-back of the abutting garage, the young man answering the door politely handed a card to the inspector with the number of the occupant's legal counsel and, after a brief call to that number, the inspector closed his file and advised the neighbor that the garage was a prior conforming use and could not be challenged.

General Strykopolos greeted Vice Admiral John Lefrak with reserve. Strykopolos had been Lefrak's technical superior at USSOUTHCOM, and he did not think much of Lefrak, although he conceded that his judgment might have been colored by Lefrak's branch of service. Lefrak in turn figured that Strykopolos was a necessary evil to the project; you needed ground capability beyond what the SEALS had to offer, personnel-wise and besides, the General had access to the President and could be the canary in the mine, an early warning system for information leak detection.

The two of them stiffly saluted Admiral Lionel Catchings without allowing their minds to drift into negative territory. Vice Chair of the Joint Chiefs, heir-apparent to the whole piñata, their clear organizational superior and recognized as totally candid, totally ruthless and totally informed about everything—no one messed with Catchings, roger that, over and out.

Admiral Catchings knew General Strykopolos from the old days before he ended up as a consultant and adviser holding President Queenie's hand and was not surprised that he had drifted into the political arena; he had been overly tactical in his own politics while still serving. And as for Vice Admiral Lefrak, well, everyone knew Lefrak was an asshole but a man who simply knew how to follow orders. Catchings neither extended his hand nor smiled.

General Carter Burbridge was last to arrive, his dress uniform crisp and jingling with medals and service bars that fought for space on his chest. The only member of the Joint Chiefs with no active role in the Working Group, invited as it was essential to make sure that the Army was fully committed and thus also compromised, Burbridge took his own counsel, did not try to hide his discomfort, and had the annoying habit of taking hand-written notes at meetings even though he had been asked none-too-gently to refrain from "creating a trail a ten-year-old could follow."

Carstons spoke first, although he was the errand boy, the grease that made the wheels turn. As the link to Congress and thus to the money, he did have his hand on the golden goose of course, so he was to be treated with noblesse oblige. He had buried Project V deep in DARPA while handling Congress, and skillfully at that. He had arranged the funding and achieved a remarkable level of security. In the last decade or so after it became apparent that the Project had legs, his contacts in Congress had been able to provide invisible funding by pumping other funding initiatives into a side pocket at DARPA. From the military standpoint, funding was always the bailiwick of others, not military men; they always asked, begged, demanded as it was their right and duty, complained when it was not robust or timely, and never said thank you because you didn't have to be polite when someone simply handed you what you had already earned.

And while Carstons was the link that kept Congress on board, he also facilitated the method of keeping the Executive unawares. A man of some skill and commitment, they would admit. Just not military and, thus, not quite all that one would want as a partner in their Project.

"So, always the good news and the bad news," Carstons intoned. "The tanker ship is a day out of Boston. The crude oil tank on the North River dock has been cleaned spotless and is filled to the top with our fluid biologic. Enough to do whatever we want whenever we want, provided of course we have transport. Military security is on the vessel, Berets, top notch. No apparent leaks." He paused, smiled and continued: "Bad choice of words. No leaks of *information*. We should be ready to deploy against any one of your scenarios by middle of next week." He paused again: "Of course, any scenario against which the Congressional group signs off. As agreed, of course. Yes."

Everyone looked at Admiral Catchings, who waved his

hand to continue.

Carstons cleared his throat. "Uh, yes, uh well as we approach our—time, uh, some rumblings, I will call them, have arisen. Nothing critical, but they had to be addressed."

"Addressed? I am quite certain that I do not like that word. It is devoid of content, Mr. Carstons. Please just tell us what is going on, so that we can assess criticality." Catchings washed his comment down with a small bottle of Perrier, leaned back in his chair, closed his eyes and made a small tent out of the fingers of his hands, flexing them open and shut in slow cadence.

Carstons could not show his annoyance at the gratuitous condescension, so he didn't, he just continued.

"Several things. All unrelated we are sure, that's the good part. The most serious of course was Dr. McCabe. At the last minute it was quite apparent what was happening. We could not take a chance, he was clearly conflicted. After two decades and ten billion dollars, well that's not the time to have second thoughts. Our doctor unfortunately was struck by a truck, a hit and run on his bicycle, and expired just last week. They never did find the vehicle that hit him…"

Carstons paused for questions but was not surprised to hear none.

"Yes, and then someone dropped a remark, a minor one to be sure, to another Senator, Senator Darwimple—he's an old man, a lame duck, on the Senate Committee that deals with technology. It got this Senator Darwimple interested, sent some staff flunky to poke around about McCabe, called the D.C. office of the CIA. So the CIA sends someone to ask Darwimple a few questions—you know how those guys are. Nothing happened from that so far, they really just have vague questions, no clue about V or even about the functionality of the program. So, it would have stopped there except," Carstons paused and allowed himself an internal sly smile, "well, I guess you, General, said something to our President and that caused her to query the FBI, the CIA and then summon Darwimple to the Oval Office to discuss the point."

Everyone snapped their attention to General Strykopolos, most notably Admiral Catchings, who rocked forward on his chair, eyes wide open, and then softly asked, "Greg? Greg, what have you been chatting about with Her Highness?"

Strykopolos, totally surprised by Carstons' report, reacted as a true warrior, attacking the messenger.

"Carstons, I cannot believe you are wasting our time with this inaccurate bullshit. The President overheard a question at a briefing, she asked me about it and got pissed when I told her I didn't know what the remark was about. I told her I'd run it down, but frankly thought she had forgotten about it." He glared at Carstons. "How did she get to Darwimple anyway?" Asking as if it was all Carstons' fault.

"She apparently asked the CIA and the FBI about it and, miracle of miracles, the CIA and the FBI actually seemed to be able to coordinate on this rare occasion, unlike the old days. The President learned about the CIA visiting Darwimple concerning McCabe, so she summoned the Senator. Closed door but, seems pretty clear they all are sharing the same questions and not only are there no answers but, also, they really do not know where to look."

Catchings sipped a black coffee. He made a very un-military slurping sound while he did it, but the slurping had stopped.

"Who said what in the Joint Chiefs meeting? Who was there, who knew what was going on and would let slip something like that in front of the President, of all people?"

Strykopolos glanced at General Burbridge, who cleared his throat once and said, "I did."

Catchings opened his mouth to speak but didn't get past the "Well I wonder…" when Burbridge cut him off.

"Listen, Catchings, I don't want to hear anything about it. It was a slip. With all this shit going on, it's hard to keep track of the subterfuge and the players. I don't want to hear your speech about it or suffer your patented sarcasm. It's done and over, right? It was a mistake, right? And don't expect an apology, it just happened."

Burbridge glanced down, then up again immediately, warming to his message and beet red all over his fat face down through his several folds of chin.

"And another thing, Admiral," this last word spit out as if it were a dirty curse, "don't seem so surprised. You play with shit, you get some stink on your hands."

Catchings finally filled the long silence. "Well, General," he almost whispered, his hands extended palms downward over the table, "I thank you for your exegesis. I suppose, Mr. Carstons, it would be best if you continued with your briefing."

"You got it," said Carstons with secret satisfaction. "Let me tell you about another thing, and, this is strange. I learned today that Panos, our man in DARPA, seems to have removed his file on our Project from the DARPA offices. I am not sure what that means, but he stuck another file in its place so that someone checking the cabinet might not see that something was missing. I wouldn't even mention it, maybe he just took it home to work on it, but putting a dummy file in there, that suggests he is getting antsy. If it weren't for the chip in the original file, or if he had made a copy and taken the copy, we might never have noticed. So there's that."

"Oh, another thing from the CIA. They had agents that had been poking around the lab for years and years; lost an agent years ago who was trying to work the lab personnel. Not sure why it was CIA and not FBI but they thought there was enough foreign connection to turn the international spooks loose here in-country. CIA control thinks there is—well someone else, someone unknown to us in terms of identity and affiliation, who also is poking around. That might be the worst aspect here," Carstons pausing to compose his denouement, "but then again this is really a vague thing, we have no information about any infiltration or efforts to, well, get into our business here."

Admiral Catchings rubbed his temples, old blond now gone gray, the only hair on his head save a silver fringe rimming the back of his skull, giving him an almost bookish demeanor and also helping anchor his military hat onto his head on those rare occasions when he went to sea as an observer. He then held up his hand for silence, leaned forward and spoke with slow intensity.

"That last item, sir, is the only thing you have said this afternoon that gives me any concern. We know that the Senator knows little. We know that the FBI and the CIA are floundering, talking to themselves. We know that the good doctor is communing with God and that God is unlikely to meddle with our program. I am sure we can deal with Panos, he is neck deep in Project V with nowhere to go. But we know there is a joker in the deck. And everyone knows that you cannot tell what the joker will do by looking at the bicycle designs on the back of the cards. That is what drives my conclusion here."

"We need to accelerate our Program. Time was never our friend but now could be our enemy. I had taken the liberty of putting the ship to sea, but at this point we need more of a statement, more of a commitment. I want you, Carstons, to tell your people to get their political ducks in a row in the next ten days. Tell them we will deploy under Plan A. Please obtain their consent."

Strykopolos started to say something but Catchings was already standing, half turned to the door.

"Gentlemen," Catchings said quietly, "I do hope that this is not the twilight of our defeat by reason of the aggregate of carelessness and a bumbling woman who accidentally became President. Lefrak, I expect you to have the military part of this spit-and-polish ready. I surely don't want to suffer defeat after all these years."

He took a couple of steps, then again turned back to his speechless audience: "And Carstons, get me the okay on our first Plan. Because, Carstons, we are going to execute Plan A whether your Senators like it or not and they cannot afford to fail to execute at their end. If they cannot deliver, we and the country, and all of them, will be compost on the shit-pile of history."

28

The harbor waters were warmed by the over-heated September and the twists of the Gulf Stream that seemed to echo the continued warming of the world. The harbor waters lapped against the piers and sea walls of Boston, a few inches higher than decades ago when McCabe first brought V to Panos at DARPA, an idea that he wanted Harvard to fund but they would not. The harbor was dirtier now than ten years ago, the higher water level and increased rainfall occasionally over-filling the Deer Island treatment plant, by-passing the dump pipe carrying sewage away from the City and into the heart of Cape Cod Bay, but still clear enough to reflect the running lights that illuminated the tanker's progress through the channels, around the airport runways, swinging west against the evening wind and making dead slow up the heart of the harbor.

Captain Anderson, retained to help guide the tanker through the harbor and make the sharp turn to port so as to align with the North River, thought all along that this was indeed a strange assignment. He was contacted privately, at his home and not through the pilot service office. The caller had confirmed that Anderson was an ex-Marine, had discussed the need for "mission security," and had advised that Anderson would be picked up and escorted to the vessel and paid the day before, in advance and in cash. The sum offered was sufficiently large to elicit prompt acquiescence and to make him understand that it would be a very bad idea to discuss his engagement with anyone.

The strangeness of the arrangement was not mitigated when he was picked up in a black SUV with government plates and accompanied by three young men in sports jackets which did little to hide their taut physical condition. The small power launch taking him alongside the tanker was unmarked but left from the Coast Guard pier deep in the harbor. It moved much faster than it looked capable of moving, planing in the water eastward towards the outer channel in disregard for the inner harbor speed limit. At one point, opposite Long Wharf, it roared past an MDC police boat which completely ignored the launch. In normal circumstances the speed and spray would have triggered a siren, a chase-down and an inspectional boarding.

"What's on this tanker, anyway?" Anderson asked the taciturn man piloting the launch, with as much of a casual air as Anderson, a blunt vet with three tours to his credit, could muster. He was met with a thin smile and told that no one on the launch had the slightest idea and that they all had known better than to ask.

The tanker itself was no surprise, a huge vessel with the usual multi-story super-structure aft, a flat façade of eight stories height, occasionally punctuated by portholes, topped by the bridge with its glass window stretching across the entire width of the ship. The level deck was crossed with a series of large pipes, some running almost the full length of the vessel. Anderson was familiar with this type of tanker and its controls, they came through the harbor every week, full with liquified natural gas, headed for the storage tanks up the North River, and left high in the water after being emptied, the lines of rust indicating on their hulls where the ships rode when laden. But this tanker, inbound though it was, rode high, clearly empty. Strange indeed.

And the mystery was heightened by the vessel's identification on its stern: "ENDEAVOR" and below that its port of registry: "NEWPORT NEWS." This ship and its port made no sense to Anderson, who had been piloting Boston for over a decade; Newport News was mostly military and in any event without Liquified Natural Gas facilities. He was further surprised—actually shocked—by the security just to board *Endeavor*. Although he had been conveyed from his apartment door through the Coast Guard base to the boarding ladder hanging off the deck, upon his stepping on the deck he was walked a few yards to his right, his credentials were checked, his fingerprints taken by a mobile device, and then he was strip-searched in the open, his nipples constricting in the chilly evening breeze.

Captain Anderson stood there and tried to think of the $10,000 in hundreds that had been delivered to him the prior day, a salve to his indignity and chill. It occurred to him that he was never going to receive a 1099 tax form in the mail reflecting that money; the money was no doubt invisible. If he chose not to report it on his tax return, Anderson was quite sure he would never be caught; at least if he had the good sense to not deposit the cash in his bank account.

Standing there and then walking towards the elevator to the bridge, Anderson was able to see, as his eyes adjusted to the low light, a double line of men standing at alert along both sides of the ship. The lines stretched out of sight towards the bow, he was quite sure the entire perimeter of the vessel was protected. The uniforms seemed familiar, also; looked like the Green Beret types he knew in Afghanistan. Better not to stare too intently, Anderson thought. Just do your job, steer the ship up the River to the tank farm, and then get the hell out of here.

Up the elevator in silence with a new escort of two armed soldiers, and just before he stepped over the threshold of the bulkhead onto the bridge to assume the helm, Anderson had one last thought, which he decided to throw out of his head as too disquieting to retain: were they going to actually put him ashore, just let him go back home, once the ship was secure? Or would he be detained until the operation, whatever it was, could be completed? Or, worse?

There were no introductions on the bridge. The personnel were all uniformed Navy, but no name tags. They were introduced generically; "this is the Captain, this is the Officer of the Watch, over there is your helmsman."

The controls were standard, nothing he had not worked with many times before. He called for quarter-speed until he drew even with the airport, dropped to dead slow, and relied on his inertia to carry the vessel through the 115 degree starboard turn westward into the middle of the inner harbor channel. Although the ship was riding high, was easier to steer and did not need the full depth of the dredged center, it was standard practice to find the deepest course; standard practice to take no chances. You centered your vessel as a matter of habit.

On the turn, the ship's clock softly rang two bells, a good time to be coming through. All the tour boats and commuter ferries would be docked for the night. Pleasure craft, including the sailboats annoyingly raced in the wider part of the inner harbor, would all be tied up and out of the way. It was impossible to steer around these obstacles, and it took over a half mile even with reversed engines to stop the tanker, so all the smaller traffic in the inner harbor was a constant concern. Even the commercial fishing boats, those few still in the water with the Stellwagen Bank fished almost into oblivion, would be either tied up at the Fish Pier or still at sea bobbing with their nets. Only an occasional police boat or Coast Guard launch could be expected at this time of night, and Anderson was sure that any such vessel was not going to find itself in the way of his tanker—not tonight.

The *Endeavor* moved in silence past the two tall residential towers to port which had sneaked through permitting, before the City had tightened its rules to protect the waterfront, past the now-darkened airport runways to starboard. It moved in silence past the restaurants and piers lining the harbor, its hull almost even with the top floors of the old warehouses long ago converted into pricy condominiums, its super-structure looking over the tops of the roofs, creating the strange illusion on shore that the buildings themselves were afloat, passing by the massive ship. They slid past the Coast Guard base, past the baseball field with its startling view across the harbor to the Charlestown Navy Yard, and past the masts of the anchored *USS Constitution*. The tall obelisk of the Bunker Hill Monument, perched atop Breeds Hill in an accident of history, stood dim in the background.

All clear. Then they came to the River, draining its narrow waters into the west end of the inner harbor, requiring a sharp turn to port complicated by the marinas on either side, particularly the large marina in East Boston with its finger docks and pleasure craft. The turn needed some boat speed, even dead slow churned a mass of under-the-surface flow out the aft end as the screws pushed into the turn and into the current, the surge of water pointed directly into the marina once the turn was almost completed.

Anderson teased the helm to starboard to permit his swing to port to clear the shoreline, then swung hard to port at dead slow. The surface of the water was calm, but the docks with their small boats and a couple of house barges began to pitch, straining against the lines that tied them. Water then drenched the dock surfaces, making them temporarily impassable. Inside the house barges, occupants used to the rocking awoke and held to their bed rails until the tanker was a couple of hundred yards up the North River.

The river was beautiful, Anderson thought, particularly in moonlight, lined with small houses, an occasional restaurant and expansive marshes on either side. But, Anderson noted without surprise, this was a new moon, there was no moonlight tonight. He should have focused on that before, this was an operation that would not be planned when the world was lit by moonlight. They passed the yacht club with its small sport fishing boats at anchor, the Riverside Inn with its incongruous windmill in the middle of its parking lot, and then through the start of oil and gas tank farms just before the river narrowed into non-navigable shallows. The *Endeavor* was bound for the very last pier, in fact Anderson had thought that the tanks at the far end of the farm had been decommissioned years ago, he could not remember the last time he was asked to pilot to this pier. Some tanks were sunk into the ground, others standing tall. His dockage was next to a large tank above the ground, far back, up a straight course to the decommissioned area.

He lined up the tanker parallel to the dock, called for reversed screws at dead slow, and watched the vessel drift gently alongside. On the dock, a particularly large complement of men in Navy uniforms grabbed the lines and began tying off.

Anderson's normal practice was to stay at the helm until the tie-off was complete, you never knew what could happen, but one of the Navy uniforms tapped his shoulder and motioned to the bulkhead. No goodbyes, no eye contact, he was out the door, down the elevator, and to his relief promptly escorted to a stairway which had been propped up along the dock even as the crew continued to tighten up the lines. To his greater relief, Anderson was ushered to the roadway, wordlessly motioned into the back seat of a small black Honda, and the car promptly pulled away, slowly navigating the pitted macadam, heading south towards Boston.

"Do you know where we are going?" asked Anderson.

"Yessir, sure do. On my GPS."

"Great. Well it's in the Back Bay..."

The driver interrupted to say he had the address, that the Uber service was careful to know exactly where each trip was headed and what the route was to be, and it was nice that time of night with little or no road traffic, people around Boston were not likely to be out late on a weeknight.

Anderson sat back and decided to relax and assume that things were just fine and that he was headed home.

He chose not to focus on his firm belief that his car was certainly not sent by Uber or by any commercial car or limo service. He did not inquire if they needed a pilot to take the tanker back down the river. He briefly thought he might take his suitcase of money and check into a hotel for a couple of days, just, you know, for safety's sake; but that also did not seem like it would fool these people if, in fact, they were for any reason unhappy with his continued breathing. It is what it is, he thought. Whatever that meant.

If you looked inside his well-worn wallet, you would see multiple identifications for Father Peter Smith, Episcopal Priest. Not a clever name but after all, he thought, the joke about everyone being named Smith worked because there were so many of them to begin with. Sort of like hiding in plain view. Nothing remained bearing the name Lyle James Vincent. Or any other name, Ivan thought. He concentrated on holding his camera, a bit heavier than the usual camera because of the night-viewing lens assembly, as steady as possible as he filmed the docking of *Endeavor* from the far shoreline, half-stooping in the reeds until his quadriceps ached.

Father Smith was not quite sure what was happening when a single civilian got into the waiting Honda; he pushed the button on the electronics that would lock onto the car's GPS and report back to him a destination in case he found later that the civilian was of interest. But his present focus was to assess the nature of the docked vessel, the number and nature of the crew on the vessel, and the large contingent of troops who had preceded the vessel's arrival by a couple of hours and had assembled both a rolling stairway and a couple of shore-side bunkers into which it looked as if some light artillery, more like mobile rocket launchers, had been installed.

Ivan was not quite sure what was happening, but he was expecting that the tanker would be riding high and empty, and he was not disappointed. The information from intercepts, forwarded by their man in DARPA, had led him to have someone monitor the sea lanes and then to pick up radio traffic. The encryptions were robust when used, but these people were sloppy; the operation was not in the clear, but enough passed without code to reveal some clues even to unsophisticated surveillance.

And, the linkage to the McCabe lab was unsettling with its possibilities. So what was going on, in fact? And what was his path to further insight?

He ran through all four battery packs and recorded all the activity on the dock until the sun started to come up. Much of the shore crew came onboard, presumably to sleep, but Ivan noted that there was an armed shore patrol perimeter and that there remained a cordon of armed personnel around the entire deck of the *Endeavor*. He also thought they had left a crew at each bunker though his view was hidden by the mud-works. Ivan slowly stepped backwards through the reeds. He did not dare stand upright but needed to move his leg muscles which were cold and cramped. He lay back on the damp narrow strand of sand and let his circulation return. He then crawled back into the reedy undergrowth and began his half-hour stooped-over hike back to his rental car.

29

Richards' office was larger than anyone else's office. As Speaker of the House, he had some perks denied most others. And, he had it swept that morning to confirm that there were no hidden ears. Carstons arrived first of course; he never was one to risk something happening to which he was not privy. An advantage, Richards supposed; it likely made his information more reliable, and in the current circumstances the quality of intelligence was very important. In fact, a matter of life and liberty.

Carstons was not his usual self; his suit needed a pressing, its vertical pinstripes crossing over several embossed folds on the back of his jacket. His shirt collar was open and he wore no necktie, the first time Richards could ever recall seeing Carstons "out of uniform" in the past fifteen years. When Richards and the others had approached him at University of Chicago, where he headed the conservative wing of the political science faculty and where his clear and forceful writings had gained silent support from a wide variety of politically interested persons, Carstons had been the epitome of the kind of academic you just had to love as a conservative exponent: young, pale blue eyes under a high brow topped by a full straw-colored comb-over, crisp business suit with striped tie that looked pure Brooks Brothers—none of that scraggly Ivy-drenched rumpled look with tweed jackets and pants with no crease.

And nothing over the intervening years had changed his meticulous self-presentation. In his years with the DOD, Carstons presented as a supremely confident young man; or, come to think of it, someone racked with self-doubt papered over with a confident image.

In those days, late Senator Jake Jacoby from Massachusetts had helped form up the "Working Group." Reaching across the aisle to selected Senators and Representatives, shrewdly identifying common ground notwithstanding the severe rhetoric of partisanship, coalescing people based on conservative religious and cultural values, Jacoby had attracted Richards and others, safely ensconced in predictable states or districts, with the idea of coalescing support and finances over time for his far-reaching and indeed dangerous scheme. A couple of other early players had died or retired, but much of the core still remained; the key leaders would be joining the meeting today, hastily called in a manner unusual for the measured pace at which the Working Group typically operated, unusual enough to attract full attendance from the invitees.

Senator Lionel Bernstein of Illinois, the only Democrat among them, was first to arrive. Bernstein was always uncomfortable at these meetings, Richards thought, as they shook hands and settled in adjacent chairs. Wrong party, and of course being Jewish didn't help.

Bernstein's attraction to the Working Group was fueled by unshakeable dedication to the Israeli cause. Particularly after the Reactor War, a brief intense firefight between Iran and Israel during which the Israeli Air Force destroyed several sites of alleged nuclear research, in violation of the multi-lateral treaty to which they were not a party, while the Israel Defense Forces efficiently cleansed the West Bank and neutralized Gaza, actions which drew together the perpetually battling branches of Islam and even united many of the dissident rebel factions right down to the Taliban. Bernstein had been grimly directing pressure and huge amounts of financing into bolstering both public opinion and the political fortunes of the Working Group election efforts.

Senator Bernstein for his part was working hard to contain any facial clues as to his thoughts.

Speaker Richards also was as opaque as they came, unreliable with facts, uncertain with the truth, to be trusted only so far as his passionate advocacy of a social compact reflecting a brand of holy conservatism once reserved for the Tea Party Republican wing. A strange bedfellow, but there was no questioning Richards' advocacy for arming and protecting the Israeli state; nor, for that matter, the similar dedication of the rest of the Working Group. Some-times strangeness in bed was the very spice of life, thought Bernstein, pleased with his sardonic thought.

Small talk seemed inappropriate and no one wanted to open the box and let out Carstons' message until the full group assembled, so people pleasured themselves with their cell phones and tablets while the rest of the group sifted in, punctuated by curt nods and quick handshakes. Senator Julio Ramirez of Texas, he of the "Texas Ditch" that made the Rio Grande and other parts of the border almost impervious at last; Virgil Lockland of Florida, as anti-Hispanic as they came under his leathered skin, bald head, stooped gait and freckled hands confirming his eighty years, thirty of them in Congress; and finally, Senator Antoine Bellaguerre, a rabid Louisiana conservative who strangely seemed to have won the affection of the people of New Orleans notwithstanding his constant propounding of religious strictures that should be made mandatory by government action; perhaps his equally assiduous avoidance of causing any such measures to be imposed on the Big Easy signaled the implicit compromise between his principles and his love of serving in the Senate.

Senator Ramirez broke the murmured chatter as soon as fellow Senator Bellaguerre got squared in his seat. A high energy man with self-important airs, clearly seeing himself as a prime candidate for leadership of the nation—whatever that might mean in the future—he was not one to waste his own precious time, when he could be out raising funds, or dropping soundbites, or introducing repetitive social legislation doomed to fail passage even with a Republican majority as well as with his own august name affixed to it.

"So, Carstons, this is most unusual. I am sure there are reasons for the high drama. I am—I am sure we all are—all ears for your report."

Carstons had planned an orderly ramp-up to his bottom line, to prepare the group, set the stage, make his message more understandable in context. But Ramirez, the fatuous windbag, pissed him off at the get-go, yet again. Okay, let's get down to it, Carstons thought.

"Project V is an operational go. Plan A."

"Beg pardon," asked Speaker Richards, his back straight, his fingers lifted off the surface of his tablet. "Go?? What does that mean, go?"

Carstons just said it, why dress it up or soften it. "Admiral Catchings is going operational. The tanker is loaded and at sea. He intends to give the order to deploy on Plan A. He told me," this was the part he feared as it was so wrong, "to tell you that you had to approve it as he was going to do it anyway."

Not any noise or objection, not yet, Carstons thus assuming it had not sunk in. And it hadn't. Senator Bernstein knit his brow, in confusion but not yet consternation. "So, Mr. Carstons, when you say that this is an, what did you say, 'operational go,' you meant that the Admiral was going to leave the dock in Boston, and put to sea for some reason? Is there a security concern here that we are not aware of?"

There was indeed a security concern, several in fact, but Carstons did not think that was the salient message.

"What I am saying, gentlemen, is that Catchings has sailed out of Boston and when the ship arrives at the target it will implement a release. A substantive action, a release that will test, demonstrate the efficacy of the—weapon."

Several throats started to clear but Senator Bellaguerre's baritone, well-known in the Chamber and on the stump, got there first.

"He cannot do that without our assent and we have not even talked about going to sea, let alone going live with this. There is so much room for advancement once we are in place. We will have leverage for, for all sorts of things domestic and foreign. This is just not the plan at all, Mr. Carstons. Surely you reminded the Admiral in this regard." The Senator glanced around at the assembled faces, seeking and receiving nods of agreement.

"Well, the reason for my emergency request for a meeting,"

Carstons said in almost a whisper, "is that that—asshole, says he is just going to do it." People started talking all at once but Carston raised his voice four ratchets and announced, "And he sent what can only be a warning to Congress that you had best back him up because, if we break ranks and this effort fails, we are all of us dead men."

Everyone stopped talking at once, and then Bellaguerre whispered, his baritone muted by his terror, "But he cannot do that without our assent, I say…"

In the following silence, Speaker Richards picked up the phone and beeped his office.

"Louisa, please see if you can reach Director Bellingham at CIA. But listen; if he isn't at Langley, ask his staff to find him and to call me on my secure line." A pause, then "just tell them it is important and the Speaker of the House needs to talk with him immediately."

Ted Richards punched the "end call" button and sat in silence for a few seconds.

"Tell me again the target A, plan A, whatever the hell it is," croaked Representative Lockland, his Adam's apple seemingly more pronounced than ever.

Richards opened the folder in front of him and looked up. "Feodosiya."

"What, what did you say?" Senator Ramirez wore a quizzical frown.

"Feodosiya. We discussed this. The Tauric Peninsula."

Ramirez again: "That is, what? A military target in the Middle East?"

Senator Bernstein looked down at the tabletop and said in slow, measured tones: "No, no, dammit! You never did pay any real attention to all this, did you? Feodosiya is in the Russian Crimea."

Several voices were heard to murmur muted imprecations as Richards' phone began to ring.

30

Some people on the destroyer's bridge chose to adopt the more informal dress now permitted by General Orders. There were Navy hoodies and plain white shirts at all stations for this shift, but Captain Quackenbush was having none of it. Coming up on thirty years, and full uniform was good enough for all that time and good enough for today. He could not say that efficiency had suffered by more casual dress, and he surely knew his officers and key crew members well enough by name and rank that he suffered no impediment in giving orders when he felt the urge, but in the back of his mind he was sure that representing his rank by uniform had an incremental value in the crispness of response, the execution of his commands.

The bridge was all electronic, the front windows down to narrow slits. The interior walls were slightly askew, a dark grey flat finish. Not surprising, because if you stood on the deck of the destroyer you would notice that everything was not quite square; the superstructure was angled downward, flaring slightly at top, and none of the corners felt like right angles. Almost nil radar profile. Standing on the deck plates, below which were the multi-warheaded missiles, you felt the unevenness of the surface for most of the ship's length.

There were no guns above-deck; if you were close enough to an enemy to need that kind of armament, missiles had blown you out of the water an hour ago.

The Captain stepped out onto the narrow landing, noting to port the coast of Corsica, dim and low to the horizon, almost lost in the haze; the line of land moved slowly up and down with the rocking of the ship. He removed his brimmed cap and felt the Mediterranean breeze rearrange his wisps of white hair, thinned but still populating most of his dome. His tanned face set off his white mustache also, and he knew he presented a classical profile to any crew who happened to glimpse him through the bulkhead.

It was on the landing that Ensign Cuddy gave him a message decoded by the communications room, and waited for instructions. Steaming west at half-speed towards the south of France, the *Terre Haute* was making desultory progress. But since it did not have to be anywhere in particular at any particular time, it was all good. The message was from Admiral Catchings, an old friend from Annapolis, but that was strange in itself, coming directly from Washington and not through Fleet. And no one at Fleet seemed to be copied. Must be an omission in transcription, thought Quackenbush, surely Fleet had been alerted to any orders.

Stepping back onto the bridge, Captain Quackenbush stood behind his panel at the rear of the room, his back leg braced casually against his raised chair, and punched the coordinates. The screen blinked and instantaneously displayed two maps, one showing the immediate ocean and one showing the endpoint of the new course.

"Can't be right," he muttered.

"Beg pardon, sir?" Ensign Cuddy had followed the Captain, awaiting a reply or a dismissive salute.

"Go back to radio and tell me if this was copied to anyone. Have them check on the coordinates also, just to be sure."

Cuddy offered a crisp salute; Quacky was a pretty formal Captain, you did not mess around with protocol at any time.

"Oh, and Cuddy?"

"Sir," with a quick turn to face the Captain from just inside the bulkhead door.

"Call me with that please. I may want to send a quick reply."

"Yes, Captain," punctuated by another salute. Never forget to salute Quacky, or you would end up with some sort of reprimand at best.

"Helm, go to slow and prepare to set a new course. Give me timing on the course I am forwarding to you now but do not, repeat, do not, execute."

A sharp "yessir" came back. The Captain did not even notice it. Why was he being sent off the coast of Crimea? That was a zone that Fleet had made clear was to be avoided, as there was no American interest in making the Russians antsy about their conquered ocean-front resort. Or indeed, about the ever-fragile ceasefire.

The phone buzzed and he picked it up, rather than letting it go to speaker. "Sir, contents confirmed and radio says no copies were sent."

Something was going on and although the Captain always paid strict attention to orders, he knew Admiral Catchings well enough to get away with a soft inquiry.

"Cuddy, reply as follows, quote: 'Understood and executing. Advise what's stirring if able.' Read back please, Ensign."

A quick nod, he replaced the receiver. "Helm, timing please."

"At full we arrive at the hold in 26 hours twenty. At flank, 22 hours, Captain."

"Very well. Execute, flank speed."

A slow veer could be felt as the Captain turned to the Officer of the Deck. "Lieutenant, may I have a moment?"

Lieutenant Brenner was one of the new Annapolis types, less clean cut, very computer dependent, not prone to small talk. He pushed back the hood of his sweatshirt as he turned and approached the Captain with a salute.

"Lieutenant, I am not sure why but we are being sent near to the Russian zone. I have queried for clarity, which may or may not be forthcoming. I want institution of continual sonar and radar, and get someone who speaks Russian onto any military frequency we can pick up down there. Oh, one more thing; starting 0600 tomorrow, I want someone on each catwalk with binoculars."

"Binoculars, sir?" Brenner tried to keep his question respectful but what could anyone see that the electronics could not pick up?

"Yes, Lieutenant. We have them below."

"Yessir. Sir, permission?" A nod. "What should I tell the crew we are looking for?"

"Something they did not expect, Lieutenant."

"Aye aye, Sir." Brenner turned away. Everyone knew you did not push ol' Quacky. Then he thought, is this an active duty development? He had never done anything other than cruise from off Haifa to the south of Spain, seven months of boredom punctuated by launch drills always ending in a stand-down. Interesting, he thought, but not something to mention to anyone just yet. Quacky was not fond of loose talk, and always elicited specific answers when he asked where that talk had started. Better to post the orders for the deck officer roster and shrug if asked for details.

Particularly since he had no details to share.

31

Deniability was beyond possibility. Deniability lay dead in its grave, at least a decade and a half buried deep. But Senator Lionel Bernstein, "Rooster" since his fraternity days at Ohio, tall and cocky and self-proclaimed ladies' man, was not prone to just say "yes" even though there was no "no" left in his arsenal.

Bernstein had demanded that Carstons tell Admiral Catchings that the steering committee concurred but needed more detail properly to coordinate. He and Catchings, just the two of them, had to meet, meet ASAP, and "get our signals straight." Truth be told, no one in the Working Group had any idea what the result of Plan A might look like. Nonetheless, they had to sell the whole thing to key members of Congress. Bernstein needed to get enough information to prime the Working Group for the task.

Bernstein also had voted to endorse Plan A, they all had, what choice was there? But his concern was not only with Congress, but also with the President. And by extension, with the Constitution. The President was Commander-in-Chief of the entire military. She was Catchings' superior. Hell, she was, in this regard, everyone's superior. If the military executed Plan A before the Working Group had had time, months or even years, to get buy-in from 1600 Pennsylvania Avenue—well, what did that mean? Looked like treason to him. Had his clear resolve, held for decades, that the nation needed a non-nuclear existential weapon, led him to the brink of destroying that very nation? No one in the Working Group had ever put the execution scenario alongside the governance scenario.

And the President, what would she do? You could believe, as did most, that she was wholly ignorant of things military. You could share the view, held firmly on both sides of the aisle, that she was a follower not a leader. But she was far from stupid and this—situation—would not present itself as a matter of subtle military trivia. Anyone could see that the President would be compelled to take the sternest of actions with respect to the military and the Congressional cabal, both to preserve the Constitution and to head off the direst of international repercussions. Putin's heirs would be end-gamed into very dangerous, unintended consequences. Unless the United States was prepared to move massively…

But surely Catchings and Carstons must have thought of this, even if the Working Group had not. Was the military compromised from the Joint Chiefs on down, systemically, completely? And if so, the Presidency would be untenable in the hands of anyone, not just the current officeholder.

What had they been thinking for fifteen years? Or, what had they not been thinking?

Senator Bernstein sat on his small terrace at Watergate, looking out over the metal railing and the green curving shore of the Potomac, as it swept past the marinas, flowing from Mount Vernon to the Chesapeake. The river flowed through the 250-year history of the country, drifting lazily past George Washington's front lawn, flowing past the White House rebuilt after the British burnt it, flowing past the marshy flats that survived the race riots of 1835, flowing past the tidal basin with its monuments of Lincoln and Jefferson and Roosevelt and dedicated to all the dead in wars to protect the nation, flowing through the city that was the seat of government of and by the people, the city of draft riots and civil rights marches and all the things glorified in the myths that Bernstein still believed were history.

He lit an Avo and sucked in the dry, mild cigar smoke; it tickled the back of his throat but he missed the acrid burn of a Te-Amo, sorry just now that he had changed brands to reflect the mellowing taste of his years. He shifted his weight, and the webbing of his folding beach chair, taken from the cottage to D.C. years before as a reminder of those days on his deck watching the boys fling frisbees in the summer heat, pushed the rubber feet a few inches backwards against the grudging resistance of the tiles on his terrace floor.

He was a dead man. Of a sudden, that was clear. Dead politically, and indeed perhaps physically also, ultimately. All roads led downward, but one was less of a steep decline to hell; one had a landing spot where some recompense might be earned. Dropping his barely puffed cigar into his onyx cigar ashtray, a gift from some Mexican admirer no doubt seeking his ear years before, the Senator walked to his telephone on his small desk in the hallway, the desk that once was in his father's dry goods business in Canton.

The Senator smiled. "How do you do this?" he asked

himself, then realized he was speaking out loud. Well, likely there is no protocol for this circumstance, but he was a Senior Senator from a large State, a member of the President's own party. Maybe you just dialed up the White House and told whoever answers that you need—expect—a few private minutes with the President on a matter of great import. He smiled again at the thought, giddy with the thought, a giddiness that appalled him. He mustered his Senatorial voice.

"I need to see the President forthwith, immediately, on an urgent matter of national security," he announced to his over-stuffed armchair.

The Senator was still chuckling as he picked up the phone, and then realized he did not know how to call the White House without ending up speaking to some tour guide. But no intermediary could be trusted. What the hell, he thought, sometimes you just gotta move forward until you get to where you were headed. He checked that he had his wallet, patting his breast pocket and feeling its solid bulk, his folder which contained his Senatorial credentials, and called down to the concierge in the lobby.

"Please call me a taxi, will you, Frank?"

32

Captain Stoneman and Colonel Detwiler had met at a party in D.C. in the summer of 2025. Each long divorced from their earlier mistakes, they found mutual sympathetic ears. One drink led to another, and next morning they found themselves in a room in the Capital Hilton with mutual ear-to-ear grins. Duty kept them in different parts of the world but they stayed in close touch, sharing carefully planned mutual leaves. Also mutual was the sense that periodic fucking beat the shit out of dealing with two Army officers trying to maintain a marriage.

Neither Detwiler nor Stoneman knew the slightest thing about tankers, hoses and fuel tanks, nor how exactly they were supposed to execute their orders to fill the tanker with the contents of the onshore oil storage tank. In fact, they knew precious little about the tanker itself; they were Army through and through. But that first morning, days before the meeting at which Carstons told the Working Group of Admiral Catchings' actions, a large van with U.S. Government plates and no other markings pulled up to the perimeter with orders assigning the 445th Engineering Company to General Spears' command. Senior Petty

Officer Leo Finkelstein had been assigned to head the deck crew which, Finkelstein advised Detwiler, had experience in fueling transfers to tankers.

Be damned, thought Detwiler but, in truth, he was not surprised. Whatever was going on was well-oiled from the top, no friction and nothing left to chance. He briefed Roberta, putting her in charge of the transfer.

"Don't know shit about this," she had protested.

"Just point to the pipes on the deck and sit back and relax," he had replied.

Finkelstein was in the Navy because it was the better choice offered by the judge in Paramus who thought it was not a good thing that he was selling cocaine to cover college tuition at Rutgers. Prison seemed the worse choice. After six years and several promotions, Finkelstein found he rather liked the service. The anti-Semitism was muted, much of the undercurrent of anger and offensive jokes being reserved for gays, trans-sexuals, and Muslims. And running in the Navy was a slow track for a fast operator like Leo; the enlisted men were mostly dumb as posts and the guys from the Academy mostly left him alone to play with his couplings and hoses. Maybe Finkelstein would make a career in the Navy, take some courses, continue to deal the drugs to the men and women who appreciated the safety and discretion of scoring their highs from a source they could trust because he had so much to lose personally if he got sloppy.

But he never mixed his two businesses, and this evening he was off-loading a tank of something into this slightly rusty vessel named the *Endeavor*. Although he had his doubts, the stern was freshly painted with the ship's name and it was the only visible part of the hull that had seen any naval paint in many a year. And his orders were even more curious, right down to arrival by car with a driver assigned from a different unit. Discovering next that the specific design of the valve heads on deck clearly belonged to a vessel on which he had served and which had the name *Lake Superior* painted on the hull, Finkelstein concluded that he was going to be smart and, for once, keep his big trap shut.

Senior Petty Officer Finkelstein had assumed at first that he was to load fuel of some sort, but that did not parse with his specific handling instructions, particularly the extremely specific instructions about spillage and containment. Rather than setting up the orange floating barriers to contain fuel spillage, or venting the transfer for explosion prevention, or capturing any ambient vapors, he was ordered to treat the transfer for potential toxicity, which made no sense since he was to take off enough of the contents of a large storage tank to fill the vessel. If the stuff inside really was toxic, he did not want to think about it. He had selected his best people for the task and done a little research about handling toxic materials. Much of that literature dealt with small amounts, perhaps a couple of gallons at the maximum. While they would be using only a few of the ship's compartmentalized tanks, they still were dealing with an estimated one hundred thousand gallons.

And the timetable was short. He reported to a female Captain who was introduced as his immediate superior, and who was in Army uniform on a naval vessel for yet another mystery, that he would start right away. He had asked if she had checked the condition of the hose connections and valves at the tank-site. The blank stare back told him all he needed to know; Captain Roberta Stoneman might be good at something other than keeping her figure as she moved towards 40, but she sure as hell knew zero about loading tankers. His suspicion was heightened by her formality; anyone who made it a point to insist on being addressed by rank with attendant salute was not exactly confident about what was going to happen next.

Finkelstein's men reported that the valves seemed a bit rusted on the outside and the threads on the outlet pipes were really in a bad way, so he spent the afternoon supervising an external cleanup and the installation of high-pressure collars which could be sealed over the hose connection as a safety measure in the event there was leakage from the coupling. He had obtained a sealant designed for biologics, to bond the edges of the collar to the pipe and hose, and was inclined to inquire further as to the mystery fluid and ask for a protocol if the collar filled with any leakage, but decided to settle for a 24-7 contact with someone in Naval Operations to whom he was told he could direct inquiries if the need arose.

"But we are counting on you, a Senior Petty Officer, not to have any such need, if you catch my meaning," he was advised at his last briefing.

"Aye aye, sir," he had replied. It was someone on the staff of some Vice Admiral Lefrak; come to think of it, an odd contact to inquire about some leak of something in an out-of-the-way, non-military facility up a river in Boston, Massachusetts.

And what's with the Green Berets, he wondered. About to walk a few yards along the shore to urinate, he was politely signaled back within what he realized was a pretty tight perimeter.

"Just going to take a piss," he had offered.

"Just piss in place, sailor," had been his reply. "We're all friends here."

There were a hell of a lot of Green Berets, now that he looked around. At intervals on deck, and all the way down the pathways to the edge of the concrete apron, and then the narrow margin of marshland. Looked like a couple of sandbag bunkers out at the edge of the jetty to the north, also. "Fuck this shit," Finkelstein mumbled.

"What did you say, sailor?"

"I said, get this fuckin' shit done," Finkelstein replied. And fast, he thought; he could feel the sour sweat forming in his armpits and up his ass; he did not like this assignment, not one bit.

He had his two best men test several couplings, each theoretically sized to fit the outlet pipes from the tank. He was feeling for the one that felt tightest, that cinched up most willingly, with the most turns indicating a better bond. He was not too worried about the hoses going to the ports on the ship, on inspection he was surprised to find some almost-new fittings and others that had been rethreaded. But the tank, that was another story. By dusk he was content with the hook-ups; he tested them by hand, then had a couple of the men pull and wriggle the connecting hoses both at the tank end and the ship's end just to give him confidence in the bond. He knew that kind of test was useless, the concern was for a few drops spilling, not that the whole shebang would give way; but Finkelstein seemed comforted in at least testing what he could test before he opened the valves.

"How are we doing?" Stoneman asked from the deck

next to him. He had not seen her disembark, but the gangway was mid-ships and he was far aft and facing the wrong way.

"About ready to let her rip, Captain."

"We are supposed to sail with high tide in the harbor tomorrow at 1900 hours. We need six hours to go down river and make the turn, we need to weigh anchor at 1300 tomorrow. How long is this going to take?"

Finkelstein had been given flow rate per hose line as part of his instructions. He needed no more than eight hours. That was a long time but the orders contemplated a very slow rate, keeping line pressure per square inch well inside spec tolerance. It was mid-evening, he glanced at his watch, it was 2200 hours.

"No problemo," he said. "Uh, no problem, Captain," he said smartly.

"Very well, Senior Petty Officer, please proceed," she had replied; and was that a very slight hint of a smile, just a tightening of her lips but with a hint of upward curve as she turned away? She really likes that Captain shit, he thought.

"Okay, boys, here is what I want. I want each line opened slowly, one at a time. We start with the A line, then B and C. First step is to secure the pressure cuff and free the valve wheel, just a quarter turn. Then tell me if you are getting any flow reading from your meter. Open quarter turns at a time until you are getting 12 gallons a minute, then tighten up to ten and let each line run a minute or two before you turn your attention to the next line. Is that clear?"

A couple of mumbles that were likely acknowledgment only elicited a loud repeat; "Gentlemen, is that totally clear?"

He counted five "yesses," assumed the sixth was buried in there somewhere, and issued his order to proceed.

It was not until a little past midnight when someone, he was not sure who, came running up to his folding chair, from which he was watching the very slight bobbing of the floating walkway across the inlet, its one bald bulb making uneven yellow splotches on the surface. "Not sure what's up, sir, but you better come quick. Take a look at the second line…"

By the time he walked the ten yards back to the piping, the edge of the seal holding the collar onto the couplings had lifted and a steady dribble of clear liquid was flowing down the plastic and dripping onto the deck and trying to reach the railing and the river below.

"Why are you just staring at it, sailor. Seal the fucking valve."

After a few seconds, "Sir, I think it's stuck."

"Get some more arms on that wheel," Finkelstein yelled. He grabbed a couple of rags that the men had used to wipe their hands and started mopping up the fluid from the deck.

Three minutes later, all hose valves shut down, Finkelstein picked up the secure land line and dialed a phone number in Annapolis. As it started to ring, Finkelstein was thinking to himself, how much of that shit actually got out, anyway? Not more than a quart or two, he guessed. He moved his crew back and yelled for the Green Berets to make a new perimeter around the valve heads.

Finkelstein wiped the moisture off his face, the sweat dripping from his nose and lips. He dropped the rags into a bucket and told himself to seal the bucket in plastic and await orders. The fluid was odorless, clear, not sticky.

He had not noticed the slight spray from the valve as the crew tightened it. He felt more sweat coming down from his hairline onto his face, and reflexively wiped the sweat across his face with the back of his hand. The sweat mixed with the residue of the spray. He grabbed his water bottle from the holder on his folding chair and took a swig. He wiped his mouth again with the back of his hand. He had been assured that, whatever was going to run through the pipes, it was valuable but in its present form harmless.

It was almost 72 hours later that he rolled off his bunk and died on the floor, his skin blotched red and his hair tufting out of his skull. His death was mysterious but not reported beyond his CO and, thereafter, to his family. By then, the *Endeavor* had cleared the Boston roads and was sixty hours east, making 28 knots through a placid North Atlantic.

33

"I can't find our tanker T330, Captain Rosser."

"What do you mean you cannot find T330. It's a tanker, Lieutenant. It's a pretty big ship to get lost."

"It is supposed to be in the yards at Norfolk, although I cannot find an order for it, Captain. I contacted the port officer and he says it sailed a couple of weeks ago on special orders from Admiral Catchings. No destination, marked covert."

"Covert? Tankers aren't generally used on covert missions, are they, Ensign? Did you call the Admiral's Chief of Staff?"

"Yes, Captain. And they say they never cut any such orders."

Outside, the sun was settling gently in Suitland, Maryland, but the office of the Chief Intelligence Liaison was windowless, hardened and impenetrable electronically. Captain Rosser squinted at his Lieutenant for a moment; it made no sense.

"You sure, Lieutenant Walker? Because if I bounce this to the satellite guys at NGIA and NRO and the ship is sitting in dry-dock we'll never hear the end of it."

Walker was out of the Academy, pretty proud of it, didn't like being treated like an idiot, he was fourth in his class and chose the Naval Intelligence Office because he had a life-long fascination with matters of cybersecurity, espionage and the use of technology to disrupt traditional modalities—including how cold wars were fought.

"I am, sir, 100% sure of this intelligence. And there is no traffic from recon indicating any alternate location. Sir."

"Thank you, Lieutenant, please just leave your report here. You are dismissed."

Rosser reviewed the papers; not many although it looked pretty thorough a search. But the tanker was listed as 750 feet in length and there was no Mayday so it was somewhere, and it was big, and so it could be found for sure.

He checked his directory and called the active mission line at IMINT to see if Naval Intelligence had any information, at the same time entering an encrypted message to the security desk at the Imaging Intelligence Systems at the National Reconnaissance Office in Chantilly, Virginia.

"This is Captain Rosser at Naval, asking you to verify me so we can discuss in the clear."

A pause, no more than ten seconds, then "Agent Charpentier here, Captain. What can I do for you today?"

"Well, this is a bit awkward. We have a report that—well, actually we don't have a report about one of our ships."

"Sorry, does that mean what I think it means, that you cannot find it?"

"Yessir and you can imagine I hesitated to place this call because, well it's pretty embarrassing the truth be told. You are not Navy, are you?"

"No, no, I'm actually assigned by CIA. So what are you suggesting? I assume you want a satellite survey? Where should we be looking? Give me the signature identification for the vessel, also, give me the code number so we can know what we are looking for both physically and by energy, infrared and electrical emissions."

"Well, sir, this is pretty embarrassing but we cannot find any orders cut for anywhere after Norfolk over two weeks ago, so you better do a computer search and pick it up there and trace it. If it put to sea directly east it could be almost anywhere by now."

Agent Charpentier rocked back in his chair. He was sensitive to the political ramifications of expending substantial resources in looking for a ship which really could not disappear and which, indeed, was one of ours.

"Maybe, Captain, you should kick this upstairs at Navy and get orders on how to proceed?"

"Sir, I don't mean to be argumentative but let me be blunt. If the ship can be found quickly in plain sight I have no interest in being the person who made a big deal out of this to my superiors, particularly since my office did the initial analysis."

Charpentier smiled. You still needed to cover your ass in this man's military; things never change.

"Captain, send me the code references for what I need and we will track your ship for you. This isn't a little bitty one, is it?"

"Sir, please. This is hard enough. And no, it is 750 feet long and its maximum flank speed is 28 knots and I really would appreciate knowing where the hell it is."

It took the computers twelve minutes of searching the satellite records to track T330 steaming out of Norfolk up to Boston and then to Eastern Ukraine where it should not have been. It took Charpentier another two minutes to report the anomaly to the Principal Deputy Director, National Reconnaissance Office at Fort Belvoir. It took the Principal Deputy Director another two minutes to advise Imaging Intelligence and Naval Intelligence that he would take it from here, and to send all the data to the Joint Defense Facility in Pine Gap, Australia, and to ask what they knew about what was going on in Russian Crimea, formerly Eastern Ukraine. It took General Victor Stoddard at Pine Gap less than ten minutes to check with his branch chiefs and bounce the matter to both the CIA/Langley and to the National Geospatial Intelligence Agency at St. Louis Center. No one reported anything unusual in the Crimea.

Satellite imaging showed that T330 was docked, there were people around and it was not making steam. There had been a fleet of oil trucks coming to the ship a day ago; intel concluded they were delivering diesel to the ship to replenish its fuel supply, although the source of the fuel was something of a mystery so far.

No one in NGIA could understand what was happening but there was no military movement by the Russians, nor by the Ukrainian forces. While infrared suggested that the oil trucks had driven around the night before, there were no known installations near where they had driven.

Agent Luis Espinoza at CIA in Langley could shed no light on the situation; he had no on-the-ground surveillance and no better information than the satellite data accessible by everyone else. His area was interpreting intelligence out of NGIA. He could not link surveillance reports about a known Russian agent, maybe named Ivan but with numerous suspected aliases, which CIA sources had placed in Boston and then presumably in Southern Russia at about the same time as T330 made its journey, as that intel came from a different department and did not cross-reference on his computer search with T330.

Espinoza wrote up the situation, which was indeed sensitive; an American military vessel, albeit only an unarmed tanker, was tied up at a remote dock in Russian Crimea in a particularly radar-free zone, and, in fact, it seemed like some effort had been made to disguise the vessel from satellite observation. Without the information that Naval Intelligence had provided, it was doubtful that any other country's intelligence would be able to locate T330 if it did not make way, unless they physically took a walk and stumbled upon it.

Finally, although he had not been asked about any other vessels, Espinoza noted that there also was an American destroyer in that same area which he had understood was a restricted zone.

Agent Espinoza's report was one of about a dozen briefings from various agencies which Mark Leopold found on his desk the next morning. A former conservative Senator and head of the Senate Foreign Affairs Committee, he assessed all reports as Director of National Intelligence, the link between all the agencies charged with intel responsibilities. President Peters was attentive to his daily briefing but she was without military or geopolitical background and he tried to limit the number of matters he included so that she could focus on the obviously critical.

Mark Leopold omitted T330 from the morning's briefing not because there was so much else of greater importance.

Instead he picked up his specially configured cell phone, a disposable "burner" but with the most recent dual encryption and a VOIP protocol that went through a certain secret server network installed by the Joint Chiefs to carry ultra-un-hackable communications between the heads of the armed service branches in time of war. A voice at the other end simply said, "What?"

"They tracked the tanker to the Crimea. Naval Intel picked it up. They can't put it together yet. But you have to figure they may. Still no traffic indicating the Ruskies are tuned in but that sure as hell is going to change in a day or two. This whole thing is going to get very public very quickly."

The voice at the other end was strong, confident, and replied without hesitation. "This doesn't matter now. The thing is done. One way or another it is going to blow wide open. I suggest you delay a day and then brief the President with what you know. No sense getting in trouble later when they investigate, getting hung up for sitting on it. You just took a day to check it out is all, then you reported it. Make a couple of calls, check elements of the file. Send an encrypted inquiry to a couple of places. Document what you are doing. And don't worry about it, we're on time and rolling."

"Hope you're right it doesn't matter."

"Will you just relax, Mark. The world is about to get much more interesting. Compared to the next few days, tracking T330 backwards from the Crimea is going to be the least of the agenda items at 1600. Get to work, I'm signing off." He put the phone down, stared out the window at the ships at anchor.

Senators, he thought. Former Senators. They're all the same, scared of a little incoming fire! Admiral Catchings relit his cigar, a Cuban Churchill, and watched the thick smoke curl up into the air ducts of his office.

Part Three
2027

34

The North Crimean Canal had gone dry shortly after Eastern Crimea was annexed in the Spring of 2014. The Russians blamed the Ukrainians for shutting it down to destroy the crops. The Ukrainians blamed the Russians for turning off the valves, killing the crops in exchange for the propaganda gain of painting Ukraine as anti-Russian. Whatever the reason, water for agricultural and civilian use dried up at the eastern terminus of Kerch, deep in the heart of the annexed territories.

Moving north under claim of necessity and cover of power, the Russian army tapped into the Canal just below Dzhankoy, reconnected the Krashohvardiiske distribution canal, built a new reservoir to tap local river waters near Novoivanovka and thence hooked that reservoir into the North Crimean Canal, establishing a patchwork of fresh water supply which Ukraine could not disrupt short of successful invasion. This de facto supply system remained in place, part of the delicate trading of interests between Russia and Ukraine which teetered on a balance of gas, oil, water, currency and guns after 2014.

On the moonless night of September 15, a convoy of tanker trucks headed out of Feodosiya driven by Ukrainian soldiers wearing Russian army uniforms, which were easy enough to obtain on the black market if you had enough Kentucky bourbon, American sex tapes and a kicker of Euros.

In Nyzhnohirskyi Raion they turned West a few kilometers to the shore of the Novoivanovka Reservoir, which was wholly unguarded and skirted by a well-graded hard dirt road. The twenty tankers parked to the left of the untraveled road around one in the morning, pulled the hoses to the unfenced edge of the water, and opened the chock valves on the trucks. In forty-five minutes they rolled up hoses and drove in orderly fashion back down the peninsula, to the small emergency storage reservoir that had been taken off-line by the Russians. The tankers were hidden in plain view, two orderly rows of army-marked vehicles sitting at the ready. The drivers got into agricultural lorries, changed back into farmer's clothing, and slowly began to roll west with their loads of potatoes.

It had been a long hard day and night; many were tired and thirsty. They would sleep when they reached home. As for their thirsts, they imbibed from large water cans they had brought with them in their trucks. The reasonably pristine rivers of Eastern Crimea, far from most industry and spring-fed for centuries, had not tempted them to drink the local water. Not this night.

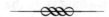

Two mornings later and forty klicks south of the Reservoir, Roman walked to the front of the tailor's shop at the fringe of the village. "I think I'll take a walk into the Center," he said over his shoulder to his employer.

Petro Novinsky was used to Roman's habits. Several times a day he would go to the town center, taking his small tankard with him. He would drink a glass or two of the fine cold water from the central pump. "It clears my body of the threads of the shop and the dust of the street," he would say.

"Don't take all day, we have lots to do," Petro said softly. He did not like to lean too heavily on Roman. They both had returned to their ancestral village after the break-up of the Soviet Union, as young men anxious to reclaim the homeland of their parents. For good or ill, they became friends, then started working together in the Fall of 1994. More than thirty years later, older and more sanguine about life, they had settled into their town and resigned themselves to being gratified by speaking the old language, not working too hard, and spending nights drinking vodka together.

"Sure, sure," said Roman as he left the shop, "I'll just be a few minutes."

Roman passed the graveyard where his wife Olga was buried, dying of a cancer shortly after their marriage. He still lived in the small cabin she had inherited, still using the same furniture and a shrinking supply of dishes, glasses and housewares. His son Stephen long ago had moved to Kiev; he visited once a year and they would share the only bond they knew. They would go to the edge of the pristine river and cast into the rapid flow in search of the large carp.

Roman reached the town center and was pleased to see Ludmila sitting on the steps of her grocery store. He filled his cup with water and sat down beside her. These days he did not sleep with her very often; for some reason it did not seem worth the effort to either of them.

"A beautiful day," he said.

"Yes it is, Mr. Sokulsky," she replied.

"Do you want me to get you a glass of cold water, Ludmila?" he asked. "You look a bit parched."

"Yes, thank you, Mr. Sokulsky, that would be nice."

He rose. "Then I will be on my way. Novinsky gets anxious if I am away too long."

The next day, the 17th, Roman was not at the shop by 9, which was his starting time, but his absence was not unusual for him. By 10:30, Petro said to himself, "Ah, another sunny day and he is off chasing carp again. He will come strolling in later in the afternoon and hand me a fish and think we are even."

On the 17th, when Roman did not appear by noon, Petro put a note on his door that he would return in a half-hour, and that customers should retrieve their own clothes from the rack and leave their money on the counter. Things were pretty informal in the village, and it was too small for anyone to do anything improper.

No answer upon his knock, Petro opened the unlatched front door as he had done many times before.

"Roman, are you here? Are you ill?"

The daylight filled the small room and Petro saw Roman's back in the bed on the far wall.

"For God's sake, Roman, get the hell up, you bum. You have all your work left from yesterday to do."

Petro walked over to the bed and gave Roman's shoulder a gentle shake. It was just enough to roll Roman onto his back, revealing a blotched face and wide staring eyes.

"Roman! Roman! Roman, can you hear me?"

Petro ran out to find the mayor. "I must remember to wash my hands," he thought. "I don't know what Roman caught, but I want to get any germs off my hands."

On the evening of the 17th people in Sevastopol and Simferopol began to feel weak and dizzy; by the next morning they took to their beds and then they began to die. A few at first, then many. In the surrounding countryside, farm families and townspeople began to feel the symptoms; but not all. Those far from the canal system, reliant on local streams or deep wells and without need for vast agricultural water supplies, seemed to show no ill effects. By the 19th it became clear that a wholesale health crisis was descending on the entire Russian peninsula; health care providers and infectious disease teams began arriving from Western Russia, and World Health Organization crisis personnel arrived by private plane with advanced test equipment and powerful microscopes.

By the next week, the dead were piled in public buildings or lying in place, and ancillary diseases, typhus and plague, began to show up in the city cores. Crimean Prime Minister Karalev swallowed hard and asked the United States to send a team from the Centers for Disease Control, as no one on-site had any idea what was occurring. The only things they could discover were that the contagion was not airborne and was wholly absent in certain areas.

The CD.C. noted similar deaths in certain cities which, on analysis, were tied to Sevastopol by airline links, and on further analysis to routes where the aircraft were resupplied in the Crimea. A careful analysis of the food and water loaded onto aircraft revealed nothing identifiable, but as a precaution plane loads of food and drink were flown in from Moscow to the airport on a regular basis.

The caregivers and researchers succumbed also, and careful analysis of their lives since arrival finally isolated the water supply as the likely culprit. Water samples were tested on all manner of animals, to no effect. No world-wide epidemic broke out, and the event was declared contained. Water samples were taken and carefully transported to leading research centers around the world for further study; two vials were sent for analysis to the newly named high-security laboratory at Harvard and were signed in by receiving at the Caleb McCabe Memorial Infectious Diseases Laboratory in Cambridge, Massachusetts.

The Russians surreptitiously brought dozens of violent criminals awaiting execution or serving lifetime sentences at hard labor and began giving them water. In a week they had a map of deadly waters that tracked almost exactly the pattern of civilian deaths on the ground. Those given water from the off-line Novoivanovka Reservoir seemed to die more quickly, although the back-up supply in that facility seemed to be clear, odorless, tasteless and unexceptional under the microscope. The Army ringed the Reservoir, disconnected it from the canal system, and began examining the twenty tankers lined up in waiting in the adjacent field. No record of the tankers could be found in Army records and the license plates and door identification numbers appeared to be fabricated.

35

"Senator Bernstein. Please, resume your seat. I am, needless to say, quite surprised but have taken your message at face value. I was about to retire but was reading... In any event... Ah, can I have some coffee brought for you, Senator? I didn't mean to seem so formal."

"No. Uh, no thank you, Madame President. I—I'd rather just say this while I can, it is difficult, and would prefer to just, you know, tell you why I presumed to, uh, well, this seeming high drama and all." Bernstein thought he could really use at least a glass of water but did not, indeed, want to delay; his throat felt dry, tight.

"Sure, Senator, then let's get down to it. What is it that you think I should urgently know?"

Bernstein had planned to just blurt out that Project V was going operational with Plan A per Admiral Catchings and without oversight from the Working Group, but as he prepared to speak he realized it was not that simple, at least if he intended to be taken seriously as, indeed, he must be. He sighed, looked down, looked up.

"Madame President, I just realized this is not so easy

or quick to say. I am afraid you will think I am deranged. It is midnight, and I just have to beg you to listen to me."

"Well, okay, Senator. I am here, I am awake and I understand you view this with great seriousness so let's just say I am yours until you tell me you are done speaking your mind."

"Madame President, this is a story that goes back two decades and involves groups in Congress, the military establishment and the intelligence infrastructure. It does not to my knowledge involve, nor did it ever involve, the Executive. The closest, as far as I know, that this matter has involved you or your office is the involvement of one of your advisors, and I am pretty sure he has taken steps to contain this information from you."

"Senator," the President said with a cold chill running through her mind, "are you by any chance referring to something involving General Strykopolos?"

Bernstein sat up straighter, his surprise evident by his eyebrows raising and the slight involuntary opening of his mouth. "Why, yes, yes it does. How did you conclude—I mean I haven't even started to tell you—well, anything concrete, specific."

Sarah Louise Peters squelched a wry smile, as this was a situation in which any sort of smile was critically inappropriate. "I am very anxious to hear what you have to say, Lionel," she said evenly.

Lionel Bernstein swallowed hard; he was not prepared to be called by his first name by the President, with whom he had only a handshake history, and he read the "Lionel" as a segue into the deep hole into which he had sensed he would be sucked by the truth. Perhaps the President had suspicions but could not possibly have the information that Bernstein was about to impart. Their meeting room was enclosed, no windows; he pictured the darkness outside, the new moon leaving the sky a dark gray, the decorative lighting from Washington's monuments and Federal buildings drowning out the sight of the stars, leaving a blank canopy, a vacuum of sights overhead. How long would the story take? Would the sun be rising by the time he walked back out of the White House? If, he thought, he would be allowed to walk out?

"Long ago," he began, then winced at the theatrical preamble but just pushed ahead with his monologue, "a scientist at Harvard had an idea that was financed by the Federal Government through various agencies, particularly DARPA. For over twenty years this scientist developed a formulation, I am to this day not sure what is in it actually, that turns the germs in your stomach, which are generally benign, into something that, well it kills you if you ingest the substance. And it is just like water, acts just like water, mixes with water. And under a microscope you can barely see the effect this substance has on the microbes in your stomach. In fact it is so subtle that almost anyone, even a scientist, is going to miss it, miss the changes it makes. And, this enzyme or catalyst or whatever this thing is, I'm told that it's so structured that it is, in effect, hidden by its relationship to the molecules of the water itself. It is, if you will, the perfect weapon for some—uh, applications."

"A germ warfare agent, Senator, is that what you are saying?"

"Well, we came to look at it as just a weapon. It really isn't a germ, more like a biologic, or perhaps a virus. It just permits the development of this, lethality, if ingested. And it doesn't pass from person to person, it just affects what is already in your body. We came to view it in just that way, not really germ warfare at all."

"I see." She wanted to discuss the distinction, the convenience of the conscience-saving choice of words, but this was not the time. "So tell me, Lionel; you refer to 'we.' Who might that be, this group of 'we'?"

Having thrown in his penny, Senator Lionel Bernstein had a sudden urge to withhold his pound. "I am afraid," he equivocated, "the 'we' is a rather large group." He glanced up to see the President lean forward expectantly. "In the military. In the science community. In the intelligence community."

"And," she gently prodded, "I assume by your presence here, in Congress?"

"Yes. Yes, in Congress. Over time that is. And the group changed a bit as people left Congress and others were elected, you know…"

"Come now, Lionel. You came here to tell me what is going on. Just tell me."

"I am involved. We have a Working Group. At least that is what we call it. The Working Group in Congress includes the Speaker, Senator Ramirez, Representative Lockland and Senator Bellaguerre."

"Quite a robust little group. Are there others in Congress who are advised, even if they are not in the Working Group?"

Bernstein had always suspected so, but Speaker Richards and Carstons were the keepers of that part of the secret. "I am not sure," he said softly.

The President shifted in her seat, then picked up the

phone next to her. Bernstein froze with fear for a moment, but the President simply asked for a pitcher of water, two glasses, and the sending of a note to her household coordinator that her return to the residence was uncertain for the night. She held up her hand for a pause until the water tray arrived, a matter of no more than half a minute.

"Do you want to take some notes on this, Madame President? There is a lot more to tell…"

Sarah did then smile briefly. "Won't be necessary," she said. Bernstein wondered if the meeting was just being recorded, or if others were listening, either from the beginning or by reason of the telephone call for a pitcher of water, if there was some code or other telltale in the way she had phrased her request. No matter, he thought. Many people were going to know sooner or later, and none of them would have much sympathy for Senator Lionel Bernstein. Perhaps not even the person who threw the switch after his treason trial.

"Okay. So the Working Group generally supervised the development and testing of the substance. We made sure it got funded, out of black box funds, whatever it took, whatever the scientist wanted or asked for, that was fine with us. We didn't even know it would work, at least in the beginning. After a while, of course…" He trailed off.

"This scientist, this man at Harvard, is he still involved, is the University still involved?"

"No, no, after a while we pulled the thing and put it into our own laboratory for security reasons."

"And the scientist? What about him?"

"Dr. McCabe. No, he is not involved. Anymore." Bernstein tried to picture the impact of the discussion on the President;

her expression was of polite interest, nothing more. She must be one hell of a poker player, he thought. "No, McCabe is out of the picture. Dead actually."

There was a pause and Bernstein realized he was to continue. What the fuck, he thought, she might as well know the depth of the problem.

"The Working Group did not order it, but I am pretty sure the military had him killed a few months ago."

"Assassinated?"

"Run over by a truck, actually."

"Almost archaic, wouldn't you say, Senator?"

It was not a question to be answered. The President waited, looking with curiosity at him. She thought back to her meeting the prior week with Senator Darwimple. Surely she was about to learn the part of the story that Darwimple could not supply, or even hint at. How deep was this, how much damage had been done, and how to control it for the benefit of the country? Volatile issues all, she thought. But she was not prepared for what followed.

"The main thing to know, Madame President, is that Project V, that is what this is called in the Working Group, is about to go live."

"Live?! What does that mean, exactly, Lionel, live?"

"I didn't approve it, mind you. No one at the Working Group wanted this, the military gave us an ultimatum."

"Lionel, you are here because this is very very serious and dangerous. We are not dealing tonight with assessing blame. I admire your coming forward, although I venture to guess that you realize what the personal cost will prove to be. So I need to know exactly what you mean, and I need to know it now. Please."

Bernstein looked down, he could not maintain eye contact. He said in flat monotone: "Admiral Catchings is shipping, I think it fair to say has shipped, a supply of this substance to the Russian Crimea to disperse it within the water supply and test its effects."

There was a very long silence. Then, "My Joint Chiefs are involved in this?"

"Yes, ma'am."

"And by 'test' you mean they are planning to kill people?"

"Yes. That is what I am saying." Bernstein jerked his head up; his eyes were watering, his shirt collar now soaked with his sweat. "Very many people."

"Holy Mother of God," said the President of the United States.

They sat silently, in two armchairs, fabric of vertical dark blue and white stripes, small red stars randomly scattered on the back of the seat, feeling the time absorb the message and suck all the air out of the room.

36

"How was your breakfast, Senator?" The President wiped a smear of egg from the corner of her mouth; she never could get used to the linen napkins with the presidential seal in the corner and insisted on Scotts paper napkins at all except formal State dinners.

"I didn't realize I was so hungry. It has been a long night." Bernstein paused. "I'm exhausted but…"

"What do you want to say, Senator? After what we shared last night, surely there is no subject too sensitive to raise."

"Yes. Well, frankly I was wondering if I was free to leave or if—well, you know." Bernstein looked down because he was afraid to look up.

"Actually, I was thinking about that, and I am not quite sure what happens next but, until I can figure that out I decided I did not want what I know to become common knowledge. So, Senator, I have a deal for you which, frankly, is not open for discussion. I am going to let you leave here and you are going to not mention tonight to anyone. And by anyone, I mean not anyone. Not to your family, not to your priest, not anyone."

Bernstein smiled. "I'm Jewish, you know."

"Then you cannot tell your rabbi. And if any more information comes to you which you think is the slightest bit interesting, however trivial, I want you to give that information to me. Do I make myself clear?"

"Yes, of course, Madame President. But—so I come to the White House and…"

"No, no, of course not. Let me just say that I will arrange a continuous mode of communication and leave it at that. And one more thing: when you leave here you may, over the next few hours or even days, begin to get the sense that people are observing you. That would be an accurate perception. Do you understand me?"

"Quite clearly." Bernstein stood and the door to the Oval Office opened and a wiry young man in tan slacks and a blue button-down shirt took a couple of steps into the room.

"Good day, Senator. And—I almost choke on these words for reasons you must understand but—thank you for coming to see me."

Bernstein nodded and took a few steps towards the door, stopped and turned. "And may God be with you, Madame President."

"She always has been, Senator. Good day."

37

The Situation Room was only half full. The Cabinet and the security advisers were standing in clusters, tea and coffee in hand, flakes of croissants floating down to the carpet like the first gentle snow. The President sat and the others promptly followed. It was never good news when they were summoned at six in the morning and particularly when admonished to not bother shaving or showering.

"Madame President, what is going on? And shouldn't we wait for the Joint Chiefs? Jesus, I'm tired."

The President liked Ginny Thieu. A lot. Daughter of boat people out of Nam, several degrees from State Universities, a storied career in the intelligence community where, notwithstanding her knowledge of five languages, her flat Asian face framed by black bangs sitting on top of a roly-poly four-foot ten-inch frame made her beyond invisible, indeed unnoticed or instantaneously discounted as irrelevant. Ginny had drifted through think tanks and the Ivy League professorship thing until recruited to the State Department a dozen years ago. Her appointment as Secretary was the President's most controversial by far, and without doubt the most successful, as the taming of truculent leaders from Istanbul to Jakarta could attest, and as to which the absence of even more difficult foreign tyrants could silently bear witness.

"There will be no one from the military joining us today."

The room fell silent for more than a few seconds. Ginny broke the tension with a loud slurp of her tea from the saucer. "I think, Madame President, you should tell everyone what you know," she whispered.

And Sarah Louise Peters told them what she knew.

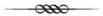

"So which approach should I use to initiate the call?" Peters had not slept for thirty hours and would have much preferred to get some rest before moving forward, but her inner voice told her to grow up and get it done. "The bat phone or through the envoy?"

The three people remaining in the Situation Room had been joined by an extremely nervous telecommunications specialist sent over from the CIA; all the White House staff trained on the hot lines were military, and all military personnel attached to the White House were sequestered in secure basement rooms staffed by the Secret Service. As no public actions out of the ordinary had been taken, replacement shifts reported and were escorted down; the plan to notify their families, pursuant to Operating Manual 24, that their family member was held for extra duty, was activated in order to give the President another six to eight hours before any inkling of an issue could leak out into the military system.

"The envoy is too slow. Period. And people are dying.

To go through the system will be bad PR." Ginny paused. "Actually bad from a humanitarian standpoint also." Her tone was almost sheepish; reference to humanitarian issues was not exactly alien to her portfolio, but also not top-of-mind.

"Bat phone it is." President Peters shrugged and asked the CIA tech to initiate the call.

She then picked up her direct line to the Security Office in the building. "Bring up Petri."

Newly appointed to Defense, Lewis Petri was a fierce hawk from the other party, named by Peters under the dual inaccurate impressions that it would silence the hawk Senators and that Petri could be easily contained.

Secretary Petri had that morning, with proud defiance, identified himself as a liaison with the Working Group, bemoaning the impetuous military for ruining decades of responsible planning by the scientific, Congressional and military communities for the public protection. Peters wanted Petri in the room; the Russian President was not going to be a happy puppy during the phone call, but also might want some details that Petri alone, within the available Executive branch, could impart, and even add credibility to the underlying narrative. What Peters would be telling Russian President Andorpov sounded more like a crackpot theory than something that had actually occurred in secret at a cost of billions of dollars over the course of two decades, in a country perceived by the Russians as rife with leaks and lack of robust security capability to begin with.

A quick tap on the door, Peters nodded to Homeland Security Secretary Tulkiwicz to open the door, and Petri walked into the room.

"What the hell is the meaning of locking us in a room and not letting us go home?"

"Well, Lewis, that is an extremely curious complaint coming from someone who might have expected to be placed in formal custody, isn't it?" Peters stared openly at Petri, who stared back silently.

"Mr. Secretary, here is what is about to happen. I am going to use the hotline to speak with President Andorpov. I am going to tell him everything I know. I am going to try to prevent a military response. Or worse, a chemical or biological response. I am going to offer him every single assistance either of us, and our advisors, can think of. I am going to tell him that I am taking steps to control the American military. If he has any questions, any at all, wherein you may be of help to either his understanding of what happened or to his remediation of this situation, I will have you speak to him. You will be factual, contrite, and helpful. You will do this immediately and without hesitation. Is that clear to you, sir?"

Petri slumped, his arms falling limp by his sides. "You're going to tell him everything? You're going to compromise decades of patriotic effort? You're going to give him the best thing since the atom bomb? Who are you to do that, to go—go—the Rosenbergs were fucking patriots compared to you! I—I won't do it. Do you hear me? And I beg you, beg you not to do it. Don't sell out your country, you—you…"

Peters arose and walked slowly across the carpet until facing Petri directly. Her face inches from his, she spoke softly, quietly and with no rancor.

"Lewis," the President said slowly and so evenly that Petri physically recoiled, "you and I have had our moments but I cannot begin to tell you how much I need your cooperation, your nonpartisan support and partnership, at this moment. You will do as I ask, Mr. Secretary. If you do not, you will find yourself immediately on an unarmed U.S. domestic aircraft headed towards Moscow. The other seats will be occupied by your wife, your daughter who even now is en route at my request from Notre Dame, and your son Tony and your three lovely grandchildren."

Petri whispered back: "You wouldn't. You wouldn't dare. You don't have the balls for it."

The President smiled. "You will have your chance to test your theory, Lewis, but I want you to know that Ginny and I agreed we would personally enjoy the moment."

As they stood there, a shrill loud ring emanated from the speaker box on the desk in the center of the room.

Everyone stared for a couple of moments, and then Ginny jumped forward to pick up the handle. She squinted in concentration, then slowly seated herself in the nearest chair.

"Yes, yes," she said. "This is Secretary Thieu," she said. "Of course, as quickly as I can," she said, and then she pushed the mute button, stood again and faced the President.

"It's Andorpov and his military senior advisors. He wants to speak with you immediately. About Ukraine. He says that his intelligence apparatus presented him with proof that the U.S. Army is planning to poison everyone in Russia."

38

"Well, at least he is calling, not dropping bombs," said President Peters as she signaled her tech to sequence the connection and recording protocols, which in turn would alert the Under Secretary for Russian Affairs that he should log onto the transcript that would be posted by voice recognition hardware almost contemporaneously. After a momentary crackle, followed by a half minute of silence, a palpable echo seemed to fill the room; the speakers in the ceiling and table activated. Almost immediately the connection buzzer went silent. Someone's heavy breathing could be sensed through the line.

"President Andorpov, is that you?"

There was a slight pause, and then a thin young voice said, "Yes, I am here, Madame President."

Not good, Peters thought; Gregor's English was passable although not colloquial, and he relied on a translator only when matter of great seriousness required a precise understanding of each word.

"It is fortuitous that you have called at this moment, President Andorpov. I am with several of my closest advisors and we were preparing to place our call to you on a very important subject."

"Madame President, in a moment I will get directly to my point but first, and forgive my asking, but are there any members of your military with you right now?"

Peters looked tellingly at Ginny.

"President Andorpov, allow me to be blunt, as we both I believe, have enough of a trusting history to do so without giving insult. There are no members of the military services of the United States either in this room or privy to this communication, nor are they aware we are speaking. This is not our normal procedure but, then, this is not a normal circumstance. Let us avoid dancing around; you are calling about the deaths in Ukraine, are you not?"

There was a silence on the line for many seconds. Peters hit the mute switch.

"They thought we would deny it, and then they would be all over us," Ginny said. "This is ugly enough without that overlay. I bet they are fighting with their military people right now about what next to say."

Peters took a drink of water, and nearly dropped the glass with a start when the green light flicked out. The call had been terminated.

"What the hell was that?" The President looked at the communications tech.

"Uh, can't be sure, ma'am. Maybe it was a technical thing, but my guess is that the Ruskies—oh, sorry, I mean the uh…"

Peters allowed a small smile. "No worries. What do you think happened?"

"I'm pretty sure that someone at their end purposely disconnected."

Peters turned to the group. "Whaddaya think? Call back?"

"Sure." Secretary Tulkiwicz shifted in his seat uncomfortably; he was not used to speaking in the Situation Room. "Regardless of how it happened, treat it as an accident. Nothing to be gained by highlighting any tension or disagreement they may be having. This is bad enough without any of that bullshit."

"Any other views?" Peters scanned the room. "Okay. Young man, please initiate a reconnection." The yellow light began flashing.

"Ma'am, when they pick up the light goes green and then there is about a twenty second delay before we go live."

Peters leaned back and stretched her legs, kicking off her half-heels. An odor-eater cushion fell gently onto the carpet just outside the edge of the table. Everyone worked hard not to notice it. Then the light went green; Peters rocked forward in the chair, paused, then spoke into the desk speaker, an unnecessary effort as the room was fully wired.

"Hello. Hello. President Andorpov? We were disconnected. I don't know if it was at this end or at your end," Peters lied.

"We do not know either," Andorpov lied in return, this time in person. "But can we continue?"

"Yes, of course." Peters lowered her voice, pitching intensity into it. "In the last two days, there has come to my attention, primarily through members of our Congress who were, I tell you, most distressed that military elements of the United States have in the last two weeks placed some sort of chemical into certain waters of the Crimea. We do not, here at the White House, know who did this or the extent of the action, but I want to assure you immediately that this was a rogue action. I was wholly unaware of the existence of this—this chemical or whatever it is. I certainly did not authorize its use anywhere, let alone in your country. That would be a foolish and provocative action, and wholly inconsistent with our ongoing efforts to pursue peace between our nations."

The line went mute for about a half minute, and then the translator came onto the call. "The President and the Russian government would be most pleased to be comfortable with that explanation, although it does remain to be seen as to the, the actual facts of the situation. Can you tell us how this could have happened?"

"President Andorpov, this is Secretary Thieu. I want to emphasize that this is viewed here as an incredibly serious event. The Executive was wholly uninvolved and we have not had any time to investigate. Our first act was to call you lest this be misunderstood."

Gregor's reedy voice replied promptly: "But it was we who called you…"

"Sir," Ginny continued, "I know you are entitled to be confused, even suspicious, but do you think the President and I were just sitting around here, with the head of—well with certain advisers and no military, on the odd chance that you would call us and we could pretend to not know what you were calling about?"

The translator again after a long pause: "No, I do not believe it. Others think this is too convenient an explanation but I do not believe it. I do not think you are that stupid to do that. I do not think you are that stupid to do this on purpose. But that still leaves us with two problems. Wait a moment."

After another pause: "First, how do we contain and explain this both within your military and within the Russian country? Second, how do we think about the ways of your country? If the military, as you say, can develop a secret chemical of such power and stealth, and move it halfway around the world without the President knowing anything about it, how does Russia ensure its security? We need to have a talk, President Peters, about how a modern government must control its people. Your democracy does not seem very good at doing that, it seems to us. We have the dead bodies to prove our point."

Peters pushed the mute. "What do you think?"

Tulkiwicz' eyes bulged with apprehension; and perhaps something akin to fear. "Stall, tell him we have to investigate. I am not sure where he is going with this. I need time as Secretary to alert the homeland security apparatus."

"And you think that stalling is the best way to keep the Russians from retaliating, even in some measured way?" Peters spoke rapidly, bits of spittle landing on the polished metal of the table and forming little clear droplets that reflected the overhead fluorescents. "What does Andorpov tell his people when word leaks out as it surely will? What does he tell his generals, for God's sake? He had to cut off the call to prevent who the hell knows what from happening. Or, the generals had the nerve to cut the call right in front of their President."

"We should talk about this," Ginny interjected.

Reaching for the button to reconnect, Peters waved her other hand in dismissal. The light went green.

"President Andorpov, are you still there?"

Gregor's voice had a smile in it: "You think perhaps, Madame President, I tired of this conversation and decided to call it a night?"

Peters declined to engage the diversion, although sensing it represented a tacit acknowledgement of the unintentional nature of the event. "So here is what we are going to do. First, we are going to secure our military chain of command. Before we investigate, before we do anything else with your country. Anyone who did this is dangerous to all of us. Second, we are going to investigate and do it openly; nothing else will satisfy you, and nothing else will satisfy me. People need to know; people need to be driven from hiding. Third, when this is all done, we will convene at the United Nations in New York, in Geneva, somewhere the world powers select, and we will discuss the safety of the world. Fourth, I am going to Moscow to apologize to your people. Their hearts will be breaking. They must know that the hearts of Americans are breaking also."

"Will you give us a moment, Madame President?" Gregor's voice was even thinner; what was happening at the other end of the phone?

Ginny broke the silent wait, reached over to hit the mute button, and hissed intently into Peters' ear, "You really want to go over there in person? Gotta tell you, I'm not feeling so comfortable with that."

"I don't want to go there. I have to go there. And Ginny, you're coming with me. And we are going to try to find one uncompromised general to bring with us."

She looked around the room and saw Petri at the far end, pretending to look at a wall map of Europe. "And I'm going to bring Senator Petri along to explain all this," she said.

Petri turned with a start. "They'll hang me," he whispered.

"Save me the trouble," President Peters muttered as she turned to the flashing green light.

39

November 16, 2027 dawned with a pink glow in the east as the *MV Cape Ray* rocked on the gentle Mediterranean swells, its USSTRATCOM flag barely aflutter in the morning breeze. An approaching launch cut briskly across the water, and then it was tied alongside and Ensign Milbrook Lancelot Chu came aboard two steps at a time. In his right hand was a small valise. In the valise was a small vial of clear liquid, filled last night from a river deep in the Crimea, rushed by U.S. Special Forces to the Ukraine office of the U.S. Defense Threat Reduction Agency.

"Sir," he saluted the Officer of the Deck, "I am to report to the bio lab. Would you please direct me?"

Captain Virginia Taylor was still in civvies sipping her second cup of hi-test when Ensign Chu stepped smartly through the bulkhead and pushed the valise towards her. "Fresh off the boat from the Crimea," he reported with a small smile at his modest pun. "What is this stuff, anyway?"

"Well," Virginia said with a return smile, "that's what we are here to find out. Thank you, Ensign. You are dismissed."

It took fifteen minutes to put on protective gear and

check into the secure bio lab. It was difficult to work in the lab aboard ship, things were always in some sort of motion and in dealing with toxic chemicals and biologics the slightest slip was a serious matter. Last month a pitch driven by a passing rain squall had tipped an improperly sealed canister of a mold that seemed to devour human flesh out of its gimballed container and the detox of the lab had taken an entire week.

Virginia unlocked the valise with the code that had been sent to her from USSTRATCOM in Fort Belvoir, and found the well-cushioned vial nested in the depths of the shredded foam packaging.

"Well, you sure don't look much like a weapon of mass destruction to me," she said out loud to herself, "but then you guys seldom do at first blush."

Six hours later, seated at her computer, Virginia reported her results:

TO: Chemical and Biological Technologies Department, Translational Medical Division, DTRA/Belvoir

FROM: Capt. V Taylor, USAF; aboard *Cape Ray*

RE: Sample 55939—Coded Crimea #1

ANALYSIS: Clear liquid, no precipitates. PH 7.2. Odor nominal. Chemical analysis of components: water, minerals normal to source region, biologics normal for regional flora. No discernable compounds other than as above. Anomaly: simple biologic seemingly non-complex and strangely hard to detect in water, identified in 12% alcohol solution and isolated and analyzed: unknown structure. Novel, and not gene-spliced (?). Rapid self-propagation. Toxicity nul. Reactions: no immediately observed effect on range of bacteria. Anti-microbial peptides: negative per MIT standard tests. Non-reactive with virus batch 1, 2. Cell permeability: high. Mechanics of interaction with human organisms: unknown. Suspect altered enzyme of unknown catalytic effect. Sample stable at room temps; divided sample and refrigerated and heated, half at 4C, half 98C. Stable all temps over four hours. Request guidance for further action/testing.

General Burwell Vance stared at the report and reread it twice. The November sun was setting, slatted shadows ribbed his desk though the trees and blinds; evenings came gently this time of year in Omaha. He rubbed his temples; he was tired, up for two days worried about the Crimea. The report did not help much.

He let out a sigh. "What the devil is this baby, anyway," he said to himself. "And what do I tell the President?"

On November 20, 2027, Air Force One approached a military air base one hundred and sixty-five kilometers northeast of Moscow. Since crossing into Russian air space it had been accompanied by six Russian MIG aircraft; by agreement, American escort planes had turned away at the border. To the objections expressed by her advisors, the President had pointed out that since she was to land in Russia in person and unguarded, what was the incremental value in making sure her airplane was safe in transit? To the suggestion that she could be seized and tortured by the Russians to extract American military intelligence, she wryly allowed that history taught that the most important military information could not be extracted from a mere U.S. President.

President Andorpov had promised personally to meet the plane but suggested that public outrage in Russia was such that landing at a commercial airport was unwise. The President's apology to the Russian people would be broadcast from a secure military location, and Russians in personal attendance would be carefully screened and assiduously searched prior to entry.

"It looks awfully gray down there." Ginny arched her back and pressed her head against the window, as if getting a clearer angle from 20,000 feet would provide useful information.

"It's late November, we are in the north, we're lucky it's not snowing." Sarah instinctively wrapped her scarf around her throat, although she was still seated in her warm airplane. "We aren't going to be walking around much in any event."

"Well, Madame President, your address to the Russian people is out-of-doors at your insistence."

"Yes, I know and I hate the cold but I thought it was psychologically important to be standing on Russian soil when I spoke." She sighed. "Right now, I'm not sure that it matters though. What do we say beyond the obvious? And we still aren't sure what it was that we dropped into their drinking water, only that we have tons of it in Boston and apparently a storage reservoir of it still in Ukraine. Such craziness." She sighed again. "Such utter insanity."

"Ten minutes until we begin our descent." The Captain's voice over the speakers was flat, unemotional.

Silence in the cabin, finally broken by Ginny asking

if Sarah wanted Secretary Petri released from the rear compartment for the landing. His guards, being armed, were not to be allowed onto Russian soil and were to stay in Air Force One until scheduled departure the following morning. Sarah would speak on television, meet with Andorpov and his entourage, share a dinner and sleep in a secure wing of the airfield.

"Sure," Sarah said. "In fact, let him see the country from a window, contemplate what is about to happen."

"Do you really think that the Russians will let him leave?"

"Well, I have Gregor's assurance. We agreed that there are so many guilty parties here that making a spectacle of just one player isn't even justice. More effective if we Americans deal with him." Sarah shuddered slightly, thinking about the long process of uncovering, indicting, punishing all the different participants in what was being labeled, simply, "The Event" by the press. Surely, gut-check time for Americans, and likely further fuel for the political schism in the United States. Half the country probably will be peeved that the military had not been efficient enough to dump all of V into all the major Russian water supplies, she thought with deep depression.

Sarah reached into her large tote bag to review one more time her simple apology; a copy had been provided to Russian authorities in advance so it could be accurately translated for the voice-over during telecast, there was no change or tweak or added thought that could be inserted at this point.

The President looked up. "Ginny, in fact have Secretary Petri brought up to me before we land. I want to talk to him again before we hit the ground."

Ginny stood with a nod, and walked slowly back across the carpeting, easily passing between the rows of cushioned swivel chairs lining each side of the main cabin. She rang the buzzer at the first security door and was admitted to the room with the Homeland Security Secretary and General Boris Levanov, newly designated Chair of the Joint Chiefs of Staff and third generation American descendent of Russian emigres to the States.

Seated near the rear of the compartment was Secretary Petri's daughter, who had insisted on accompanying her father although she refused to speak with him or be alone in his presence. Her eyes were swollen from crying. In her jacket lapel she wore a pin depicting two doves in flight. Ginny sought her eye to afford a supportive smile but failed to make contact.

Lastly Ginny passed the unarmed military aides manning the President's communication system and code boxes and reached the second security door accessing the rear of the aircraft, which normally housed the President's private quarters but now had been refitted to accommodate Secretary Petri.

She buzzed, and a metal cover on the inside of the compartment promptly unlatched, allowing occupants to identify through a triple-thick lead crystal window who was seeking entry. A sharp click unlocked the connecting door and Ginny stepped inside. Petri was seated in the last armchair.

"The President wants to talk with you," Ginny said. "Please come forward with me."

Petri looked up, calm and straight-lipped.

"Is it true that my daughter in on this plane?" he asked.

"Why, yes it is. She insisted, actually."

Petri clenched his eyes for a brief moment, then looked up with a tear poised at the corner of one cheek.

"Damn you, you fucking morons." His voice was a low hiss. "And damn her and her damn fool conscience."

He glared up at Ginny. "You know," he said, "it did not have to end this way."

Ginny was about to think that such a trite and obvious thought was surely beside the point when Petri reached down and seemed to be twisting something on his right trouser leg.

The blast threw Ginny and Petri and the two security guards right out the floor of the plane, and they fell straight down towards the ground in what seemed to be a choreographed ballet.

The sound startled Sarah and as she turned to the back of the airplane the nose began to drop downwards towards the dark green Russian farmland below.

PART FOUR

FALL 2031

40

"Now it says here, section 331 of the indictment, that you had a—well, intimate relationship with this man, this fellow Harry Simpson who was killed and allegedly with the CIA. Can you tell me about that? Just in your own words."

She looked down into her lap, the way embarrassed people often do. Her hair had been straightened, and there were a few flashes of grey caught in the angle of sunlight coming into Sam Harding's law office through the partly drawn shades. In the late fall, the Boston sun was low in the sky, and the office was always filled with errant patterns.

"I never knew anyone with that name. Do you mean Barry Thompson?" There was diffidence in her tone but her eyes stayed locked on her clasped hands, tightly entwined in her lap like a schoolgirl being reprimanded.

"Of course, of course. We went over that at our first meeting. He was a spy, after all." I caught myself, again assuming whatever was in the government indictment was correct. All too often, those facts were, well, not quite accurate, leave it at that. "Or, alleged to be a spy. At the time he was using a different name, yes here, Barry. Can you tell me how you met him? With that name, of course."

The woman breathed deeply, her shoulders lifting and falling twice as she stoked up her energy. Her head slowly raised; her clear brown eyes were sharp and angry, and they reached out to me unabashedly now, aimed by the point of her aquiline nose.

"It was a long time ago, maybe eight years. I was working in the lab, just like it says in that—document. I met this guy, there weren't a lot of Black men who were part of our social group, I do not remember the circumstances. We sometimes went out for drinks after work; maybe he just joined our group, I don't truly know."

"All right, I understand. Now do you recall when this was, what year, what time of year?"

"It had to have been in '22 or '23, it was after I had been at the lab for a few years. I told you that I don't recall exactly how we first met."

I pretended to study my paper because I did not want her to get defensive and fail to answer my next question.

"And did you in fact have an intimate relationship with this man?"

There was a long silence, and I kept looking at the papers on the table in front of me until I picked up my head in response to a shallow sigh. Ms. Flowers was looking straight at me, a narrow grin almost capturing her mouth.

"You know," she replied softly, "I almost said 'how should I remember, I slept with so many guys, it was the time,'— but ya know, I was something of a conservative person. I really haven't had that many relationships; even now, sorry to say. Yes, we slept together, in my apartment or his, a few times. He was very nice, you know." A deep exhalation, a downward glance. "Then, he was just gone. No one knew anything more about him."

Another pause, then: "It was hurtful, actually…"

I let the moment sit, let the memory process out. Meanwhile I dug out the photograph relating to the third count in the indictment.

"Now let me ask you some things about someone else. Are you ready, are you up to it?"

"Sure, I assume we have to do this."

"So this is the photograph they have given us of another man, whom they have identified as Ivan Illyanovitch Petrovsky, although the indictment says that he has used the names of Allen Parsons and Lyle James Vincent and Father Peter Smith and probably many others. Do you recall ever meeting him or talking to him?"

"I saw that picture before. I don't remember ever meeting him but you know, he does look familiar. They say he was a spy for the Russians, right? And my Barry, he was a spy for us? I don't understand what this is all about."

"Well, you know what they are saying. They are saying that this man, this Russian, killed the man you knew as Barry and that you had something to do with that."

"What do they say I did?" She was all alert now, some incredulity in her voice. "Why would I want to hurt Barry? I was—well, involved with him."

"That, Brianna, is not altogether clear. I think much of this indictment is what we lawyers would call a fishing expedition. But there are several things we can surmise and none of them are very pleasant to contemplate. For example, they might allege that you contacted this Ivan and helped him kill Barry."

Brianna stood and walked to the window, looking out at the older deco building across the street which now had blocked the sun entirely from my office, plunging the street below into a dingy gray that might be pre-dawn, or post-dusk, or just what approaching winter looked like all the time in Boston.

"You know, I used to be angry and then I was confused. Now I am simply just plain sad. Depressed is a better word. It feels so hopeless. How can you defend yourself against someone with a dark mind making guesses without regard to what happened when they do not even have a clue as to what happened? Do you think you can make this right? I really have to rely on you here…" Her voice trailed off in wistfulness.

"We will defend against these charges fully," I intoned, but saw her face still engaged mine with a pleading expression.

"And," I felt compelled to continue without regard to my own apprehension, "I am quite sure we will come out fine. There is, after all, just a bunch of almost decade-old circumstances tied together with unproven guesswork." Her face then went blank again, as if she had withdrawn into diffidence.

This was the most bizarre of the defenses to which I had been assigned, no affidavits or investigation, and the complaint just a draft of a scenario which felt wholly fictionalized. I did not tell Brianna of my concerns, that these days you could not predict things, not that you ever could in courts, but particularly with the new, so-called Security Courts.

I also did not share with her another disquiet I felt about this case. It was the pictures of Simpson. Since I first saw the file I had been bothered by how familiar that face seemed to me. The other day it finally came to me. I was pretty positive that it was the face of someone who collapsed on my front steps about a decade ago.

This was not an epiphany I was about to share with Brianna, nor indeed with anyone else. These days, it was the kind of thing that could get you in trouble; the kind of thing that could get you indicted, a fleeting proximity to any small element of the long and now-often-recited history of "The Event" which led to the new Global Security Protocol. And, more than almost anyone else, having seen the underbelly of the new judicial beast, I wanted nothing more to do with it.

I had been assigned by the Bar Association, under Homeland Security Protocol 107, to the defense of Tier Three Participants, although the military prosecutors always referred to my clients as "anarchist traitors." Under the Protocol, each law firm with fifty or more attorneys was required to assign one lawyer to work for the Participant Legal Committee, defending the accused against charges brought in the new Court of Examination. Charges were propounded by indictment from the Joint Civilian-Military Committee, to which the President reported under the new governmental structure.

The firm was required to increase our last pay rate by 20%, to assign us until the Court announced our release, and to provide such legal research and facilities as any decent defense lawyer might request. As could be expected, law firms long ago having become economically rational business units, my firm had assigned one of its least productive and profitable partners to the task; after all, profits must be maintained to bear the burden imposed by the Protocol.

I first met Brianna Flowers in the fall of the year following the adoption by all fifty States of the Revised Constitution. A demure woman of color, plain but pleasant looking, she was charged with Major Contribution, a capital offense but typically resulting in a long prison term. These days, more and more tenuous cases were presented with capital ramifications. And who knew the likely results? I was preparing the defense carefully but with little confidence. In the closed venues of the Security Courts, with no public access, no press and no transcript released to the defense or public, not only what had happened long ago remained shrouded in confusion; what happened at trial also partook of the lack of clarity that comes when the standard has shifted from "can the State prove guilt" to "can the accused prove innocence."

How do you prove that something never happened? This was my mountain to climb; and, in my prior cases, a steep slope it had indeed proven to be.

41

"All rise."

It is the traditional way to call court to order, but in the Court of Examination, popularly called the Security Court, it was sort of a waste of time. Aside from the stenographer, there were only five people in the small room without windows in one of those box-like super-secure buildings that had been erected near the Homeland Security Offices around the country, so that transporting prisoners to trial was as secure as possible. Aside from myself and Brianna Flowers, and the bailiff, a beefy, burly crew-cut type who was clearly present to prevent violence unless perpetrated by the bailiff himself, there was the prosecutor, a dour-looking small man named Boxleitter who carried an odor of cheap bath powder, and the Judge.

And it was Judge Ruth-Anne Remis, with whom I had experience a couple of times before. Bad experience... She was one of those people who could sense when you did not like her. This was unfortunate in my case.

I think describing the proceedings is a disservice to the record I am making. You had to be there; a friend of mine smuggled out the secret government transcript of Brianna's trial on a flash-drive which I had converted to text on the underground market, as all officially available computers are connected to Homeland Security and are swept for improper content daily. There are, thank goodness, seemingly some computers out there that still have not been "conformed."

OFFICIAL RECORD OF THE HEARING ON THE INDICTMENT OF ONE BRIANNA JOSEPHINE FLOWERS, NEGROID, HELD AT BOSTON, MASSACHUSETTS DECEMBER 4-5, 2031, BEFORE REMIS, R. A., JUSTICE.

[The Court] "Is the prosecution ready to proceed?"

[Mr. Boxleitter for the State] "Yes, your Honor."

[The Court] "And is the Defense prepared to proceed?"

[Mr. Harding for the Defense] "Your Honor, with respect, if I may approach the bench prior to replying?"

[The Court] "Oh, there are just a few of us here, Counsel. No need for formality. Why don't you tell me what's on your mind while at your place?"

[Defense Counsel] "Well, your Honor, it has to do with the materials that were made available to me as Defense Counsel. Actually more about what I did not receive. It actually involves the Prosecutor's Office. If I could—well, your Honor, I am really not comfortable having this conversation this way and would, um, respectfully request permission for a side bar or perhaps a minute in chambers?"

[The Court] "Counsel, with all respect to you, our task here is the protection of the Homeland, not whether you are comfortable. I have scheduled this procedure for one hour and prefer you to say what you will from where you are standing."

[Defense Counsel] "Your Honor, one hour? These charges are serious and carry penalties of incarceration for long periods of…"

[The Court] "Off the record, please."

Transcription stopped 9:02 am.

Transcription resumed 9:04 am.

[The Court] "The Prosecution may call the Government's first witness."

[Defense Counsel] "Your Honor, on the record the Defense respectfully reserves its rights to object as to the time being allotted to hear this matter."

[The Court] "Reserve your rights to what end? As you know, the Emergency Protocol for the Efficiency of Justice does not contemplate appeals from the judgment of this Court. Now I suppose we could have a debate right now about the niceties of all this but bearing in mind that we have a one hour time window and that the government must get its full 30 minutes to present, all you are doing at this point is wasting your own defense time, as all of this colloquy is charged against your limit. Do you wish to discuss your reserved rights further or may we proceed?"

[Defense Counsel] "My apologies to the Court. Counsel, you of course may proceed."

[Mr. Boxleitter] "I call as the first witness in this matter Mr. Robert Licatta."

[Witness is seated] "Sir, would you please state your name and current address?"

[Witness] "Bob—Robert Licatta. I live at 18 Lawrence

Lane in Acton."

[Mr. Boxeitter] "That is Acton, Massachusetts?"

[Witness] "Yes, yes; sorry."

[Mr. Boxleitter] "Could you please spell your last name for the Court reporter."

[Witness] "L_I_C_A_T_T_A."

[Mr. Boxleitter] "For the record, would you please note that Mr. Licatta has agreed to cooperate with the State and the State has waived the optional oath of truth-telling under the Protocol favoring cooperating witnesses. Now I ask if you were ever employed at the Cambridge Laboratory of Professor Caleb McCabe?"

[Witness] "Yes, sir."

[Mr. Boxleitter] "And during approximately what period was that, what years?"

[Witness] "Let's see. From the summer of 2017 until, well I left in December of '23, took a job with, well a pharma company."

[Mr. Boxleitter] "And are you acquainted with the defendant, Ms. Brianna Flower?"

[Witness] "Yeah, sure."

[Mr. Boxleitter] "And do you see her in this courtroom today?"

[Witness] "Well yeah, she's right over there at that table with that other gentleman in the grey suit. Hiya, Bree."

[Mr. Boxleitter] "Will you please only answer my questions and please do not address the defendant, nor in fact anyone but the Court?"

[Witness] "Oh, sure. I am… well, sorry."

[Mr. Boxleitter] "Quite all right. Must be a shock to see Ms. Flowers still walking around at this point, wouldn't you say?"

[Defense Counsel] "Your Honor, I must object. Not only is that irrelevant but it is suggestive of guilt based on the witness' subjective state of mind."

[The Court] "Mr. Licatta, are you in fact surprised to see Ms. Flowers still walking around free at this point?"

[Witness] "Uh, well I haven't seen her in a long time and I'm not really sure what the thing is that is going on here. I mean the Prosecutor told me that Bree is accused of some crimes against the State but I really don't know how to…"

[The Court] "Sir, I admonish you to answer my question. Are you or are you not surprised that Ms. Flowers is still walking around free?"

[Witness] "Uh, well I—guess in the circumstances it is a little surprising given what the Prosecutor told me."

[The Court] "Thank you, that answers the question. The witness was asked if he was surprised. He has confirmed he was surprised. Your objection is overruled."

[Defense Counsel] "Your Honor, I am at a loss as to how to respond. You have suggested that I should not make any objection which of course I will abide by, and I am sure your Honor will give all evidence the weight and only the weight it deserves, but still I do not understand what relevancy…"

[The Court] "You seem to be having a bad day, sir, in my Courtroom. We have been here a scant ten minutes, one sixth of the total time available to you, and all we have learned so far is that you personally are both uncomfortable and confused, and furthermore you are suggesting that this Court is not capable of evaluating this matter. Is that in fact what you are suggesting, Counsel?"

[Defense Counsel] "May we go off the record, your Honor?"

The Court nodding yes; transcription stopped 9:10 am.

Transcription restarted 9:12 am.

[Mr. Boxleitter] "Now, Mr. Locatto, turning your attention to the time period in which you worked in the laboratory and knew Ms. Flowers, was that because she worked there also?"

[Witness] "Yes, she was there when I arrived and also when I finally left. And it's Licatta."

[Mr. Boxleitter] "Thank you—uh, beg your pardon?"

[Witness] "My name is Licatta, not Loca—whatever you pronounced."

[Mr. Boxleitter] "Oh yes, so sorry. But let us continue. Now, you went out drinking with the defendant a lot of times. Isn't that correct?"

[Witness] "Well, after work we had this place we sometimes gathered."

[Mr. Boxleitter] "That was a pretty frequent event, wasn't it?"

[Witness] "Well, yeah I guess."

[Mr. Boxleitter] "This place it was a public bar, wasn't it?"

[Witness] "Well, it was a bar, yeah. It wasn't a club if that's what you're asking."

[Mr. Boxleitter] "Yes, that is what I was asking. Now, sir, was your laboratory a secret government facility?"

[Witness] "Ya know, that's a good question. At the beginning it was just a regular research lab. Lots of them around Harvard and MIT. But at one point we showed up and all of sudden there was more security. And then there were biologic precautions, ya know? Had to scrub and shower and there were no visitors. Level Four, that's the highest level. Even though we were in the basement, if you get my meaning?"

[Mr. Boxleitter] "Yes, yes I do. Most secure level. And the government maintained security there, didn't they?"

[Witness] "Well, someone did. There weren't any soldiers around if that's what you're getting at."

[Mr. Boxleitter] "Well, something could be a government facility without soldiers, isn't that right?"

[Witness] "Yeah. I guess."

[Mr. Boxleitter] "And did not members of the U.S. government visit the lab regularly?"

[Witness] "Not sure, now that you ask. There was this guy who came by pretty often to speak with the professor and Doctor Creepy—oh, no, I meant Dr. Creeley, he worked with Professor McCabe but we were never introduced."

[Mr. Boxleitter] "Well let me ask you this. Were there a lot of expensive machines, equipment in the lab?"

[Witness] "Oh yeah, you bet. Particularly as time went by. All sorts of expensive stuff, stuff you only read about most times."

[Mr. Boxleitter] "And to your knowledge, did any other labs at Harvard have that kind of equipment?"

[Witness] "I didn't get to see a lot of the other labs…"

[Mr. Boxleitter] "But those you did see and know about, were any of them outfitted that expensively by the University? To your knowledge?"

[Witness] "No, can't say as they were, actually."

[Mr. Boxleitter] "When this nameless visitor came to confer with the Professor, isn't it true that you folks in the lab referred to him as a spooky guy? Didn't you used to agree he must be from the government?"

[Witness] "Well, yeah we talked about it, but we weren't told…"

[Mr. Boxleitter] "But you all assumed he was from the Federal Government, isn't that right?"

[Defense Counsel] "Your Honor, I am not objecting. But I request that the Court consider that that question asks for assumption, asks for an assumption held by other nameless people, asks for state of mind, asks for a conclusion as to which there is no offered evidence and no basis established, asks for hearsay and even if answered in the affirmative has no probative value. I ask the Court to strike the question from the record and to direct the witness not to answer."

[The Court] "Well, sir, I never knew that any one innocuous question could be so objectionable on so many bases but it strikes me as acceptable and, given our short time frame here and your obvious need to preserve time for defense, I will allow the question. I am asking Counsel for the State to refrain from overtly leading questions on direct examination, but I will permit the witness to answer."

[Mr. Boxleitter] "You may answer the question. Didn't everyone in the lab assume the money and the machines and the move to a Level Four facility must have been funded by some branch of the Federal government?"

[Witness] "There were lots of Federal grants floating around, you know, but—well, yeah, you could say that."

[Mr. Boxleitter] "Thank you. Now I ask you if you were present in this public bar when the defendant was picked up by the man in this picture that I am showing you."

[Defense Counsel] "Your Honor!"

[The Court] "...Well, I agree on that one. The Prosecutor will cease leading this witness and will refrain from assuming conclusions and from using derogatory descriptions of the behavior of the defendant."

[Defense Counsel] "I thank the Court."

[Mr. Boxleitter] "My apologies to the Court. We will therefore do this the long way. Mr.—uh—yes, Licatta, I show you a picture of a Black man and ask if you have ever seen this man before."

[Witness] "Sure, that must be an old picture 'cause he looked just like that maybe ten years ago when I first met him. His name was Sampson I think. He was Bree's boyfriend."

[Mr. Boxleitter] "Ah, and do you recall how Bree first met this Mr. Simpson?"

[Witness] "Oh, right, Simpson. I'm not 100% certain but I think they met the first time in the bar we were talking about."

[Mr. Boxleitter] "Oh, was he employed at the lab or by the bar?"

[Witness] "No, don't think so."

[Mr. Boxleitter] "Do you know where he in fact did work?"

[Witness] "Well, maybe I heard it but I can't be sure. Don't remember anything about that now."

[Mr. Boxleitter] "All right, understandable. But tell me this, was the defendant having sex with this Simpson character?"

[Defense Counsel] "Your Honor!"

[The Court] "Yes. The witness will answer if the witness knows."

[Defense Counsel] "Your Honor, how could he know the answer to that? The question calls for conjecture, assumption. There is no proof, no foundation for that question."

[The Court] "I am trying to give your client every opportunity to defend herself but this is just the first witness and we are not done with direct. So, I instruct the witness to answer. If the witness has an opinion or recollection."

[Witness] "Well, ya know I didn't exactly follow them home…"

[Mr. Boxleitter] "So they left together?'

[Witness] "Well, yeah, I think so."

[Mr. Boxleitter] "All the time?"

[Witness] "After some time, I think so."

[Mr. Boxleitter] "Didn't everyone in your group think they were having sex together?"

[Witness] "Well of course there was talk but, well it was their business you know."

[Mr. Boxleitter] "What was their business?"

[Witness] "The sex thing."

[Mr. Boxleitter] "Honestly now, at the time didn't you

yourself think they were having sex? Maybe you didn't say it out loud. You're clearly a polite and kind man. But if I were in the bar with you when they left to go home together and if I had asked you, like a friend, 'hey you think they gettin' it on?' would you not have agreed they were having sex together?"

[Witness] "Well, you put it that way, I guess the answer is yes."

[Mr. Boxleitter] "Thank you, sir. The State is done with direct examination of this witness."

[Cross examination by Defense Counsel] "Good morning, Mr. Licatta. I am Brianna's attorney. I am just going to ask you a few questions. I ask you to answer them truthfully. I assure you that under our system of law you need not always agree with what is allegedly true if you do not believe it to be true. You do understand that, do you not?"

[Witness] "Yes, sir."

[Defense Counsel] "Good. Now for starters, have you been charged with any violation of law in connection with this case?"

[Witness] "Well, no not really."

[Defense Counsel] "Then, has anyone from the Prosecutor's office suggested to you that since you were connected with the Lab that was related to "The Event", that they might want to look into what you were doing?"

[Witness] "Well, we did discuss who was doing what. If they looked they wouldn't find I did anything wrong, you understand? They just told me to tell the truth so I did. I still do."

[Defense Counsel] "Did the Prosecutor ever tell you that

if you appeared in this case as a witness that they would not dig any deeper relative to your history at the lab?"

[Mr. Boxleitter] "Your Honor, I object to this implication."

[The Court] "Yes, that is quite enough. Defense Counsel, this is not relevant to what the defendant is accused of doing. Please move on. Do you have any other questions for this witness?"

[Defense Counsel] "Yes, your Honor. I will be brief. Mr. Licatta, did you ever hear the defendant speak against our country?"

[Witness] "Why, no."

[Defense Counsel] "Did you ever hear her discuss any complaint with this country with her Barry?"

[Witness] "No, sir."

[Defense Counsel] "Did you ever hear the defendant say anything favorable about the Russian Nation?"

[Witness] "No, I did not."

[Defense Counsel] "Can you recall a single instance in which you recall Ms. Flowers, in that bar or at the lab or any other time, ever discussing politics of any nature?"

[Witness] "Do not."

[Defense Counsel] "And did you ever hear the defendant discuss, with Mr. Simpson or anyone else, except within the lab and in the pursuit of her duties, the nature of her work in the lab, or what she thought was being developed in the lab?"

[Witness] "No, sir."

[Defense Counsel] "Did you ever observe the defendant angry with Barry, or look angrily towards him perhaps when he wasn't looking at her, or ever hear her say anything bad about Barry?"

[Witness] "Well, once about his cologne she said it made her sort of queasy."

[Defense Counsel] "Aha. But other than that?"

[Witness] "No, don't recall anything like that happening."

[Defense Counsel] "Thank you. No further questions."

[The Court] "Mr. Boxleitter, redirect?"

[Mr. Boxleitter] "No, your Honor, don't think that will be necessary."

[The Court] "Very well. The witness is excused. Does the State have more?"

[Mr. Boxleitter] "Yes, your Honor. The Government calls the defendant to the stand."

[Defendant seated. Not sworn in under Protocol 56, to protect from future perjury offense.]

[Mr. Boxleitter] "Good morning, Ms. Flowers. How are you doing today?"

[Witness] "Well, okay I guess."

[Mr. Boxleitter] "I am going to ask you a few questions and you can just relax and tell us the truth. Is that alright with you?"

[Witness] "I always tell the truth."

[Mr. Boxleitter] "That would be good. If you tell the truth here today, we will all get along just fine. Now, for the record, would you please tell the court reporter your full name and where you reside?"

[Witness] "Brianna Josephine Flowers. That's

B_R_I_A_N_N_A. I live at 1992 Lancet Road in Framingham, Massachusetts."

[Mr. Boxleitter] "Thank you. Now, Miss Flowers—it is Miss, is that correct?"

[Witness] "Yes."

[Mr. Boxleitter] "Miss Flowers, let me ask you if… excuse me, you know this just feels so formal, would you mind, would it be alright if I just called you Brianna?"

[Witness] "May I ask my attorney if that is proper?"

[Mr. Boxleitter] "Really? Well, it is just a matter of common courtesy, but if you cannot even answer that simple civil inquiry without conferring with your lawyer we are not going to have a very pleasant morning here."

[Witness] "Well, it is just that, in the circumstances, I don't feel like I want to be on a first name basis with you, to tell you the truth."

[Mr. Boxleitter] "We established you are going to tell me the truth so you need not add that. Since you are so intent on conferring with your counsel even relative to the use of your given name, let me ask you, Miss Flowers, whether in preparing for your testimony today you conferred with anyone to help create this testimony. For example, did you happen to meet with Defense Counsel?"

[Witness] "Why, yes, I—is there anything wrong with that? I thought I could have a lawyer here."

[Mr. Boxleitter] "Oh yes, of course, but if you would please refrain from asking questions and concentrate on answering them we will get along much better. So, tell me, Brianna, how many times did you meet with defense counsel before coming here to testify today?"

[Defense Counsel] "Your Honor, can I ask you to please instruct the State to afford my client the common courtesy of using her name while addressing her?"

[The Court] "Miss Flowers, is in fact your testimony that your first name is Brianna a truthful statement?"

[Witness] "Of course it is."

[The Court by hand motion permitted the State to continue]

[Mr. Boxleitter] "So, Brianna, please answer my question."

[Witness] "Which question was that?"

[Mr. Boxleiter] Your Honor, may I ask you to please instruct this uncooperative defendant to at least answer the simplest of questions without having a fight over it?"

[The Court] "Brianna, do you understand what the State is asking of you, which is to answer the questions that were asked of you?"

[Witness] "Yes, Judge. I just got confused. I—uh—what was the question I was to answer?"

[Mr. Boxleitter] "Oh, for God's sake. The question is how many times did you meet with your lawyer before this hearing?"

[Witness] "Ah, I think five or six. Not sure, it's all pretty confusing going through this process."

[Mr. Boxleiter] That many? My my… Well, let's start at the beginning then, shall we. Can you recall your conversation that first time you two met?"

[Witness] "Some of it, I guess."

[Mr. Boxleiter] Very well. And can you now tell us what

was said by each of you during that conversation?"

[Defense Counsel] "Your Honor, I want to…"

[The Court] "Sir, spare us the soliloquy. I know what you are about to say, I have heard it from your own lips before in two or three other cases. And you know my position, so why you keep raising this point is beyond me. This is not requiring the defendant to incriminate herself. This does not deprive her of counsel, you have served that function it is quite clear. This is not a privileged communication under the Protocols as you must by now be aware. If she is telling the truth, as she has told us she is doing, then presumably you heard the same facts, as her lawyer, as she will recite today. So we just want to compare what she told her lawyer to what she is going to tell us here. Is that a problem? Tell me why that is a problem. I have indulged you mightily up to now, with such waste of time that it is clear, consistent with a fair trial, that we will have to reconvene for yet another hour at some convenient additional date. This is a great inconvenience to the Court and to the orderly administration of justice, but I do not wish to prejudice your client with your own stubbornness and ineptitude. Now, Brianna, I want you to simply answer all the questions that counsel for the State is asking you with no further ado. And none of this 'can I talk to my lawyer' business. It is clear you have met with him many times before, to the apparent great cost of the State which I point out is paying half of your legal bills to make sure you are treated fairly. Do I make myself clear?"

[Witness] "I—uh, I hear you but am not sure what I am supposed to say. Judge."

[The Court] "A simple 'yes' will suffice."

[Witness] "Then, okay, Judge—yes."

[The Court] "Very well. Defense Counsel will be seated. The State may continue."

[Defense Counsel]" Your Honor, since we are at a break and discussing the conduct of the trial, I might at this time note for the assistance of the Court that my client has appeared here and is testifying of her own volition, although not required to in fact testify under the Constitution's Fifth Amendment, an Amendment I would point out, with respect, not voided by any of the International Protocols approved by our Congress, nor in the Revised Constitution, nor voided by any internal Protocol. I would request a recess at this point to discuss with my client whether, in the circumstances, she would prefer to refrain from giving testimony."

[The Court] "Well, I was never convinced but that that Amendment was superseded by Protocol Nine, but that is neither here nor there. By appearing in the first instance, she has waived any right she might have had to refrain from speaking. And I might add that such is a fortunate development for your client, for in this case I would have ordered the administration of the serum of speech if she had declined to testify. But I do note that your hour is just about up and we are not even done with the Prosecution's case. In the interests of Justice, I will reconvene this Court tomorrow at 4 in the afternoon for one additional hour. I order the defendant remanded to the holding cells at the Homeland Security building next door until that time."

[Defense counsel] "Your Honor, she is not a flight risk. Your Honor can you at least allow me to visit with her?"

[The Court] "I do not think that will be necessary. She

has seen far too much of you already, and at taxpayer expense. Bailiff!"

"All rise. Court is adjourned."

42

OFFICIAL RECORD OF THE HEARING ON THE
INDICTMENT OF ONE BRIANNA JOSEPHINE
FLOWERS, SECOND DAY

[The Court] "Well, I am running a bit behind, it's already almost 4:30, so let's get this show on the road. We are on the record. Mr. Boxleitter, you were in the midst of direct of the defendant. You may continue."

[Mr. Boxleitter] "Thank you, your Honor. And good afternoon, Brianna. I hope you slept well."

[Silence; witness does not reply.]

[Mr. Boxleitter] "Well, okay, let's get down to it. Your first conversation with Defense Counsel, what was said?"

[Witness] "We reviewed the indictment. I told him it was totally untrue. I never would assist in the death of anyone. My whole life was dedicated, is dedicated to saving lives, to curing sickness. And he, Barry, he was a really good friend of mine, why would I want to ever harm him?"

[Mr. Boxleitter] "We understand your stated view, Brianna.

The facts are that he was killed by a Russian spy once that spy learned about the work in the Lab and people have identified you as someone who had contact with that spy. The facts are that your Barry was an agent of your country's government and he was drugged and drowned and you were the person who made that happen."

[Defense Counsel] "Your Honor, those are just the allegations. Are we not here to determine the facts?"

[The Court] "Indeed we are, Counsel; of course we are. But these are the allegations by the government and are to be given very great weight in the Security Court. Everyone who is guilty tells us 'I didn't do it.' What are we supposed to do, just tell them 'oh, okay, so sorry, you are free'?"

[Defense Counsel] "I understand, your Honor, but counsel for the government is stating these as established facts and…"

[The Court] "Sir, you are doing it again and I am quite tired. Please just sit down. Mr. Boxleitter, you may proceed."

[Mr. Boxleitter] "Please answer."

[Witness] "I did not know this Russian person. I did not know Barry was a spy. I never did those things you said I did."

[Mr. Boxleitter] "Well, you were having sexual relations with this Barry, were you not?"

[Witness] "What has that got to do with it?"

[The Court] "Now wait one minute. First, I see Defense Counsel is standing up. Please sit down. Second, you know by now that you are not to ask questions. Third, please answer the question."

[Witness] [pause; witness is wiping her eyes] "I was.

We were in love. There is no crime in that."

[Mr. Boxleitter] "And would you tell the Court how many times you made love? On how many occasions and how many times you had sex during each of them?"

[Witness] "What has that got to do with anything?"

[Mr. Boxleitter] "Now the Court has warned you not to ask any questions, Brianna. Just answer mine please."

[Witness] "I—I cannot remember."

[Mr. Boxleitter] "Well, I understand that, coming from an alcohol bar and in the heat of the moment. But can you give the Court an estimate, a 'guess-timate' if you will."

[Witness] "I don't remember."

[Mr. Boxleitter] "Very well. Now please tell me at your first meeting with Defense Counsel everything that he told you."

[Defense Counsel] "I have instructed my client that she need not answer that question."

[The Court] "Counsel, we have been through all that. The witness will answer the question."

[Defense Counsel] "She is not going to answer, your Honor, on advice of Counsel."

[The Court] "Brianna, please look at me. Good. Can you see and hear me?"

[Defendant nods assent]

[The Court] "Brianna, I order you to answer that question."

[Defendant crying—off the record 4:39 pm.]

TRANSCRIPTION OF COURT RECORDING OF
BENCH CONFERENCE HELD SECOND SESSION,
SUFFOLK COUNTY SECURITY COURT, DECEMBER
5, 2031 [REMIS, J. PRESIDING]

[Remis, J] "Counsel, why are you the only attorney who gives me these problems? By now, you must know what the new laws provide. Your client is part of a cabal that almost brought us to a nuclear war."

[Defense Counsel] "With respect, your Honor, that is only alleged. In fact, my client was only a lab technician. She had no greater role. She was, in effect, without a clue."

[Remis, J] "Does not your argument assume the conclusion? Why, pray tell, do we even bother having a trial, then? Why don't we just tear up the indictment and turn her free?"

[Defense Counsel] "That's not a fair characterization, your Honor, because that is not the alternative. And to my point, what has that got to do with my client's sex life? I ask your Honor to instruct the Prosecutor to refrain from pursuing that line of questioning."

[Remis, J] "Why do you think that is prejudicial? I am the sole judge and jury under the Protocols; do you think that I am unable to fairly render justice because my, my puerile instincts will be so aroused?"

[Defense Counsel] "Your Honor, that is not the point."

[Remis, J] "The point, Counsel, is precisely that. Perhaps if you were loyal to your country's laws and not to your client…"

[Defense Counsel] "My loyalty must be to my client,

your Honor."

[Remis, J] "We will deal with the question of your loyalty at a later time, sir. Right now, I'm hearing a case against a traitor who probably doesn't even deserve to be represented by you at government expense. Enough of this. Back on the record."

Transcription resumes 4:46 pm.

[The Court] "Let the record show that on advice of Counsel the witness will not answer any questions about comments made to her by Defense Counsel. On inquiry, this is her position as to all of the numerous meetings held by these persons. The Court is referring Defense Counsel to the Homeland Security Disciplinary Committee for Lawyers, Judges and Prosecutors for disciplinary action. This hearing will continue. Mr. Boxleitter, proceed."

[Mr. Boxleitter] "Quite a way to demonstrate your innocence of this murder. But we shall continue. And please do stop your sniffling and weeping and heaving your shoulders. The only people impressed by all that are you and your Counsel. I'll wait until you are ready. All you are doing is crying through your own lawyer's time to defend you. [pause] Now, are you quite ready to proceed?"

[Witness] "Yes I am."

[Mr. Boxleitter] "Good. How long have you known Ivan Illyanovitch Petrovsky?"

[Witness] "I already said I did not know him."

[Mr. Boxleitter] "Well at one point you said he looked familiar. Did you see him on television or in some other bar?"

[Witness] "I don't recall but I have seen the face before.

I said so all along. I cannot remember how. I don't know him; forget about him please."

[Mr. Boxleitter] "Well, we really aren't going to do that, are we? It will go easier on yourself if you just fill in these pieces here. When did you first meet him, Brianna? Did he come to you through your control, your contact?"

[Defense Counsel] "Asked and answered. She did not know him. Would the Court please ask the Prosecutor to move on?"

[The Court] "Let the record show that the witness refused to answer a direct question, seeking confirmation of a key factual element even though that element is contained already in the indictment. You may proceed, Mr. Boxleitter."

[Mr. Boxleitter] "Thank you, your Honor. The way this has been going, I think there is little to be gained by this hearing. May I suggest that the Court call for summations at this time?"

[The Court] "You'll hear no objection here. Defense Counsel?"

[Defense Counsel] "Am I to understand that the State proposes to rest its case? Because if that is what is being proposed, then I will waive my questioning of my client and consent to going directly to our summations, your Honor."

[The Court] "A wise choice, Counsel. So let it be noted for the record that both parties now consent to summations. Mr. Boxleitter, you might..."

[Interrupted by Defense Counsel] "Your Honor, now that the evidentiary stage of the case is closed, the defendant hereby moves for dismissal of all charges. May I be heard on this matter, Judge?"

[The Court] "I cannot imagine what your point might be, but I will give you two minutes."

[Defense Counsel] "Your Honor, thank you. Our judicial system always has assumed innocence until guilt is proven. The Protocols, I grant you, now place the burden of proving innocence on the defendant. But that burden arises only when the State has presented evidence of guilt, some proof that demonstrates, or even just hints at, the guilt in committing an identified act.

The State here has failed to prove anything. Mr. Licatta, if fully believed, testified only that my client had a relationship, yes even a sexual relationship, with the deceased. Lots of people have sexual relations without arranging for the murder of their partner. Nor did he link my client to the alleged Russian perpetrator by meeting, act, deed, communication—no relationship was shown. No intent, no motive was suggested. And we pass the significant issue that there is no proof that this Russian even committed the murder, if there even was any murder to begin with. There is also no direct testimony from anyone that my client was politically active, spoke of the lab to any unauthorized people, or indeed did anything whatsoever that would lead anyone to connect her with the drowning of her friend, even her lover, in a town pond at a time when there is not even an allegation that my client was present or of which she was aware.

Defendant must prove innocence but the State must at least prove some link between the act of murder and the defendant, other than that they knew each other. Otherwise, anytime one's friend or spouse was killed, that would make a prima facie case for the prosecution of the other friend or spouse."

[The Court] "Counsel, your motion is denied. There are allegations of guilt in the indictment. Ms. Flowers here has not disproven them. Under the Protocol, if the State has enough evidence to allege guilt, the defendant has the burden to prove the negative. We will go to our summations."

[Defense Counsel] "Your Honor, are you saying that this woman must affirmatively disprove, in one or two hours at most, all allegations contained in a document when there is no evidence of guilt produced in a courtroom?"

[The Court] "You try my patience, sir. I already have referred you once for disciplinary review. Let's not tempt the addition of the charge of contempt of justice, and in a Security Court at that. I will hear no more about it. Mr. Boxleitter?"

[Mr. Boxleitter] "If it please the Court, and as the Court itself has so succinctly and yet elegantly noted, defendant has utterly failed to rebut all the material allegations. She has not produced evidence that she did not know the Russian spy. She has not produced evidence that she failed to direct that spy to the place and at the time that this Russian spy slew a loyal American, who by the way was her frequent sexual partner, by drug and drowning and strong blows to the skull. She did not take any action to stop the work in her own laboratory, which she conducted for almost a decade under the supervision of the deviant madman McCabe, which led to "The Event" which almost caused a world war of enormous consequence for all of humankind and particularly for those living here in the Homeland by reason of Russian counterattack. We have learned she is the kind of person who frequented alcoholic bars and slept with men whom she did not even know, men not properly introduced, which may have been the custom of the day but still is no justification for the action. Under the Controlling Protocol that those of guilt relative to "The Event" must be punished to the extreme as a lesson to the future, the State asks for the ultimate penalty for Brianna Josephine Flowers."

[The Court] "For the Defense?"

[Defense Counsel] "Your Honor. I am compelled to say that I am speechless. Yet speak I must, regardless of consequence. Where this indictment came from I have no idea. How my client's name became related to the alleged but unproven killer is not revealed. The record we were given has not only no name of an accuser or of any witness, no dates and no alleged specific actions, but just the bare allegation that Brianna arranged the death of her friend. We cannot even understand why. It is merely alleged she was a friend of or involved with the Russian spy, although without proof or even allegation that she had any interest in the spy's country or political causes. There is absolutely nothing even mentioned that relates Barry's death, even if indeed Brianna arranged it, let alone to the occurrence of "The Event" many, many years later. I am confident that your Honor will render a judicially sound judgment on my client so that we will not end up with a rule of law where any accusation is taken as fact and where every defendant by definition is presumed not only guilty of a crime but also of being an enemy of our Homeland which we all love."

[The Court] "Thank you, Counsel. Bailiff, will you please take the defendant into protective custody pending my rendering a judgment next week. Will Counsel please remain in the courtroom? Thank you."

Bailiff and the accused leave the courtroom.

[The Court] "Let me start with you, esteemed Defense Counsel. I am not sure… Wait. Court reporter, you still taking notes? The proceeding is concluded. You are dismissed."

Off the record 5:12 pm.

43

SAM HARDING'S POSTSCRIPT

That was my last case. I refused to take any more, particularly since the Disciplinary Panel assigned me to three months of further training in the Protocols of the International System of Homeland Security and caused my firm to halve my salary. I resigned that summer.

My friends, the few I told of these developments, said that it was dangerous to resign, but I didn't much care after they hung that poor woman for no reason.

I learned from news and reliable rumor about some of the history of the lab, the involvement of the government, and the military revolt that led to "The Event" in the Crimea. I saw from the press how the Protocols came to be promulgated and how they became mandatory international law, to prevent any country from again imperiling the safety of the planet. The idea that such things, mere laws, can control the nature of man, his evil and dark xenophobia, is to my mind monumentally naïve. But so be it; we all have our failures, and the more people there are involved, by definition the more failures there will be.

I wrote the summary of her trial on a manual typewriter,

and transcribed what happened in the courtroom from the transcript my friend smuggled to me. In these times, I would not dare go out and procure a writing device which was not wired into the Master Identifying System. We all know what happens when you write something that is not subject to scan in MIS, and you are discovered. So, the most common mistake is to buy an old typewriter.

I found an old typewriter in my attic. I was fearful of running out of inked ribbon; that is an item that is not really available anymore, but if my ribbon expired I thought I could find some old carbon paper, and I could make do by constructing something out of that. And I typed this on the backs of old documents so there is no record of my going out and buying too much paper.

I have included in this narrative of the trial the facts as I recall them. To speculate on occasion as to motivation or as to matters which seem important and logical, although not directly within my personal knowledge, is an indulgence you must afford me. I also ask the reader to forgive any perceived inconsistencies. Such are my disclaimers.

The trial narrative is now complete and in good time. My last roll of typewriter ribbon cost me $1450 dollars and getting it on the off-market scared me to death. You never know who the hell you are dealing with these days. I'm going to be okay; I saved a bunch of money from all that extra pay as a defense counsel, and my kids all have jobs and have avoided the craziness of the times, so my wife and I, we'll be all right.

My biggest risk arises from the mere possession of this transcript, which I do not want to be lost. I have the vanity of thinking it an important testament. Right now there is just this one copy. I am almost tempted to re-copy it all by hand just for safety's sake. Finding a duplicating machine which is not rigged up to the central MIS security computer for content analysis is simply not possible, and one scan of this document in the wrong hands and I'm in a cell in one of the incarceration centers in Boston Harbor until the cows come home and there aren't any cows around here.

So I may try to get a visa to go to Canada and see if someone up there can print this for me; Canada is of course a party to the new international Protocols, as they are mandatory of all nations. But the government there is thought to be a little less—how to say it—a little less *thorough*. Perhaps I will change some of the details so it isn't so obviously about me although, given the facts and details, any effective camouflage will not be easy.

I am actually very emotional about this whole thing. I have no idea what to entitle this trial record, and I have neither need nor desire to have my name associated with it. But I am sure of one thing and that is the dedication page:

To Brianna. A victim of her times.
December 28, 2031

Character List
(alphabetical)

Captain Carter Anderson	Pilot service, Boston, ex-Marine
Gregor Andorpov	Russian President
Bailiff	Beefy
Senator Antoine Bellaguerre	LA, religious conservative
Director Bellingham	CIA
Nash Berenson	Russian agent impersonating a reporter, fake ID, visitor to Lab, collaborates with Lyle/Ivan
Senator Lionel Bernstein	IL, only Democrat in Working Group, Jewish, "Rooster"
Boxleitter	Prosecutor, dour, small
Lieutenant Brenner	Officer of the Deck
General Carter Burbridge	Army, Wife Letitia, Joint Chiefs

Peter Carstons	DOD, funds black op, Bethesda, visits Lab regularly, arrested, knows congressman on military budget appropriations
Admiral Lionel Catchings	Vice Chair of Joint Chiefs
Agent Charpentier	Senior Director, Imaging Intelligence Systems
Ensign Milbrook L. Chu	US Defense Threat Reduction Agency
Doc Joe Creeley	Friend of Harding, Dr. "Creepy", McCabe's principal assistant
Ensign Cuddy	Navy
Senator Lionel King Darwimple III	AL, Republican, Special Oversight Committee on Science
Colonel Lou Detwiler	Army, Fort McNair, D.C., aide to Spears
Agent Luis Espinoza	CIA, Langley
Senior Petty Officer Leo Finkelstein	Navy, Rutgers, dealing drugs at College and in Navy, died on ship
Brianna Flowers	Black, worked for McCabe in Lab, Level 4, Toyota SUV, arrested & tried at end
Frank	Concierge

Lilah Greenberg	Young lawyer assigned to CIA Office, friends with McCarthy
Guatemalan gardener	Deported after finding body of Simpson, Aug. 2023
Lois	Wife of Sam Harding
Sam Harding	Attorney, Civil Liberties Union, Newton, MA, Defense Counsel in Trial
General Roger Heathcote	Army, friend of President's deceased husband, Denver
Senator Jake Jacoby	Deceased, "Working Group"
Agent Heinrich Johnston	CIA control for Simpson
Prime Minister Karalev	Prime Minister of Crimea
Vice Admiral John Lefrak	Navy, deputy commander USSOUTHCOM
Mark Leopold	Former Senator, head of Senate Foreign Affairs Committee, now Director of Naval Intelligence
General Boris Levanov	New Chair of Joint Chiefs, Nov. 20, 2027
Bob Licatta	Co-worker with Brianna
Lieutenant	Aide de camp of Heathcote
Virgil Lockland	Representative, FL, 80, anti-Hispanic, Senator 30 yrs
Loftons, Sarah & Larry	Neighbors to McCabes, moved unexpectedly

Senator Maximilian Looper	aka Lord Looper or Loopy, Sarah Peters formerly his aide, then wife
Louisa	Richards' secretary
Ludmila	Grocery store owner, friend of Roman
Dr. Caleb McCabe	18 Windwood Circle, Newton, MA, Harvard Biological Research Annex (classified), wife Susannah, 2 sons
Susannah McCabe	Wife, 50, French lit. major
Lt. James J. McCarthy	White aide to Senator Darwimple, Yale, Academy, Naval Intelligence
Petro Novinsky	Tailor shop owner
Dr. Lance Panos	MIT, Orders from DOD, Interface with Carstons, Special Deputy Director of Project V
Sarah Louise Peters	President, widow, NYC, Art Hist. major, Barnard, Democrat, was aide to Senator Maximilian Looper (Loopy)
Laurence Peterson	Office of Intelligence Oversight
Secretary Lewis Petri	Defense, Republican, liaison with Working Group, wife, daughter at Notre Dame, son Tony, 3 grandchildren

Ivan Illyanovitch Petrovsky	Kiev, Komsmolskaya Square; aka Allen Parsons, aka Lyle James Vincent, 16 Windwood Circle, Newton, MA; aka Father Peter Smith, kills Simpson
Captain Quakenbush	Navy, 30 yrs in service, destroyer, "Quacky"
Senator Julio Ramirez	Wife Cynthia deceased, TX
Judge Ruth-Anne Remis	
Ted Richards	Speaker of the House
Captain Rosser	Navy, Chief Intelligence Liaison, ONI
Bob Sherman	Cousin of Mr. Harding, lawyer
Harry Simpson	aka Barry Thompson, 41, Black, Cambridge, CIA, watches McCabe, befriends Brianna, born in NJ, went to Rutgers, CIA recruited out of univ, Rutgers Swim Team, drowned in Newton, MA
Father Peter Smith	Episcopal priest, aka Ivan
Roman Sokulsky	Tailor shop employee, wife Olga deceased, son Stephen, Kiev
General Rupert Spears	Army, 1 star

General Victor Stoddard	Joint Defense Facility, Pine Gap, Australia
Captain Roberta Stoneman	OTS with Detwiler, Army
General Gregory Strykopolos	
	US Army-ret, killed at fishing camp in Sitka, Advisor to President Peters, fishing guide Louis
Captain Virginia Taylor	USAF, *MV Cape Ray*, Nov. 16, 2027
Ginny Thieu	Secretary of State, Asian, Vietnamese, Ivy League Prof., Intelligence Community
Secretary Tulkiwicz	Homeland Security, Under Secretary for Russian Affairs
General Burwell Vance	Omaha, Chemical and Biological Technologies Department, Translational Medical Division, DTRA/Belvoir
Carlos Vincente	Master Sergeant, Green Beret
Lt. Walker	Academy, ONI, aide to Captain Rosser

Organizations referenced:

455th Chemical Brigade (USAR), Fort Dix

Acquisition, Technology & Logistics Agency

Combatant Commands in the Dept. of Defense:

USCENTCOM—U.S. Central Command
USNORTHCOM
USSOUTHCOM
USSTRATCOM

Senate Armed Forces Committee

LOGRON 2, Norfolk—Combat Logistics Squadron 2

DARPA—Defense Advanced Research Projects Agency

NGIA—National Geospatial Intelligence Agency

NRO—National Reconnaissance Office

ONI—Office of Naval Intelligence

IMINT—Imagery Intelligence

Imaging Intelligence Systems

MIS—Master Identifying System

Afterword

The Event was written by accident based on the only "fact" in the whole book which is true: one day a man rang our bell and we found him collapsed on our suburban front porch.

I recounted the incident, and several dear friends observed that it sounded like the start of a great story.

I agreed and then asked if any of them knew of an old best seller named *Naked Came the Stranger.* My recollection was that it was written by many people, each one of whom wrote a chapter and passed the manuscript on to the next writer, and so forth until it was finished. The book was assigned an invented sole author's name: Penelope Ashe. (By the way, it subsequently became a movie as bad as the book, and you can learn more at the ever-knowing Wikipedia.)

None of my friends had heard of the book but they purported to love the idea and, poor souls never having themselves struggled at the craft of fiction, each swore to participate if only I would write the first chapter. Thus challenged, I figured I would copy the action/spy thriller genre and banged out an approximation of Chapter One, and dutifully circulated same with the simple inquiry "who wants Chapter Two?"

Following a long silence even after several further prods from me, I concluded that these newbies needed more guidance and so I wrote something like Chapter Two and resubmitted my challenge, seeking the hero of Chapter Three.

By now the astute reader will anticipate what next happened: my friends went back to their day jobs and never wrote a word, I got angered and swore to myself that I would teach them a lesson, and in order to teach that lesson spent about a year messing around with this ill-formed idea in order to bring to you, the reader, this story; and further, hoping to bring to my would-be co-authors the shame of recognizing their abject individual and collective failures.